KT-140-718

Lincolnshire
COUNTY COUNCIL

COMMUNITIES, CULTURAL SERVICES and ADULT EDUCATION

This book should be returned on or before the last date shown below.

SBI

To renew or order library books please telephone 01522 782010
or visit www.lincolnshire.gov.uk
You will require a Personal Identification Number.
Ask any member of staff for this.

EC. 199 (LIBS): RS/L5/19

McCRACKEN IN COMMAND

The Union forces were taking a beating and orders came for retreat. Colonel Brubaker and his troops abandoned their position, but Captain McCracken mistook the retreat order and held his ground. McCracken's men ended up routing the Confederates, making Brubaker look like a fool. The paths of the two men once more crossed, at an outpost in Sioux country. Brubaker knew that McCracken was going to make one more mistake — a last, violent one, courtesy of Colonel Brubaker.

Books by James Keene
in the Linford Western Library:

SEVEN FOR VENGEANCE

JAMES KEENE

McCRACKEN IN COMMAND

Complete and Unabridged

LINFORD
Leicester

First published in the
United States of America

First Linford Edition
published September 1995

British Library CIP Data

Keene, James
    McCracken in command.—Large print ed.—
Linford western library
I. Title II. Series
823.914 [F]

ISBN 0–7089–7759–6

Published by
F. A. Thorpe (Publishing) Ltd.
Anstey, Leicestershire

Set by Words & Graphics Ltd.
Anstey, Leicestershire
Printed and bound in Great Britain by
T. J. Press (Padstow) Ltd., Padstow, Cornwall

This book is printed on acid-free paper

1

A COLUMN of cavalry or infantry would have stayed on the regular trail flanking the river, but Captain Robert Duward McCracken could not risk it. Not with a battery of horse artillery trailing him in flank column. Not with four loaded sutler's wagons tucked between the double row of caissons and limbers. Yet Captain McCracken's choice of route was not entirely tactical. And his men understood this, as well as his officers, who had served with McCracken long enough to know of the uncertainties that dogged him. In the sutler's van rode the colonel, who journeyed to a new command, and he too understood Captain McCracken's choice of route.

Captain McCracken turned often in the saddle and studied the column strung out behind him. He could find no fault with interval or march rate, yet the ratknaw of uncertainty never left him. During the twelve years of living with *U.S.* on his blanket, he had never been quite able to shake this feeling. In spite of an almost fanatic devotion to detail, he seemed destined for failure; the sum total of his military service was one of average achievement; no amount of effort seemed to raise him above this rut of obscurity.

The smooth road to the south would be better than this fetlock-deep grass and the rolling hills. Better because there were no difficult fordings to make, fordings such as McCracken's command had been making at every creek. But McCracken felt that the road was too close to the mountains and too close to the river. At times his column was hemmed in between looming walls, with each twisted defile a potential womb of ambush. The infantry could use the road if they liked, McCracken decided. The infantry could fight at bayonet point if it had to. And the cavalry could close with pistol and saber. But if he were forced to fight, he would need range; and judging by the way things were shaping up, it appeared that a fight was in the making.

This was the second day of a five-day march. The second day of Indian smoke, and mounting hostiles on the ridges flanking the column, hanging out there like a half-uttered threat. The second day of nervousness and tension, eroding the command's discipline until every hillock blocking their view was a separate and nerve-wrenching worry more profound than the one before.

Lieutenant Gustave Borgnine was in command of the second section, and at Captain McCracken's hand signal he rode forward. "Continue the march, Mr. Borgnine. I'm going to take a ride through the column." He meant to sound casual, trying to create the impression of complete calm in the teeth of approaching disaster.

"I feel like a crippled duck on a mill pond," Borgnine said, his mallet head swinging to scan the ridges. He was a keg-chested man, his shoulders as heavy as an oak bole. His face was flat and heavy jowled and, although he shaved daily, the density of his beard left a bluish cast to his jaw.

"We'll fight if they close in," McCracken said. "In the meantime, they're not hurting us by watching." He wished silently that he possessed the kind of oratory that could build confidence in his command. He had served under officers who had that gift, men who could stare into the eye of devastating odds, sniff at a nosegay, then charge to victory. Twice, when McCracken had attempted this kind of bravado, he had only ended up in the field hospital with his forces routed.

"They're making me nervous," Borgnine conceded. "And, Captain, no one's ever fought horse artillery against the finest light cavalry in the world."

This was no junior officer exercising his mouth, McCracken knew. Borgnine

4

had been with him ten years now, through the good years and the bad; but the bad years, to McCracken's way of thinking, outnumbered the good. Borgnine had only been a sergeant when he went along to Edward's Ferry in '63. That had been General Gorman's Brigade, the 7th Michigan, two troops of Van Alen's Cavalry, and Putnam's Rangers. But Borgnine had learned the awesome power of artillery during those days, and the lessons stayed with him through the years, making him now a very capable artillery officer.

Still trying to ease Borgnine's mind, McCracken smiled and said, "Mr. Borgnine, you're forgetting that this is the best battery in the world." This had a hollow sound, like something a father might say to quiet the fears of a child; McCracken was instantly sorry that he had said it.

For a moment it looked as though Borgnine were not going to take the remark seriously, then his heavy face wrinkled into a smile. "You don't have to worry about this battery, sir."

McCracken wheeled and sat his horse to one side until the fife and drum section, the guidon and flag bearers pulled past, then he broke in ahead of the first section and rode between the moving caissons to the rear.

One hundred and seventy men, eight of the newest artillery pieces; all this was his responsibility, a responsibility few commanders would have wanted, yet he had asked for this. In fact, even begged. A man had to learn about himself, to find out once and for all whether or not he was a failure. Colonel Truman Brubaker, in the sutler's van, would have been glad to settle the issue for McCracken; he had a distinct dislike for the captain, and was typical of men in positions of authority whose own talents are limited but expect nothing less than genius of their subordinates.

Dust rose thick about McCracken, raised by the heavy wheels of the gun carriages and tons of limbers and wagons, each pulled by six horses. Not the pared down cavalry mounts, but heavy draught animals, capable of tremendous power.

From the rear of the column, a horseman rode forward at the gallop, nearly running McCracken down as he sawed to a halt. He was a dark-haired man with bold, glistening eyes above a neckerchief tightly stretched to keep out the dust. He wore a tan corduroy coat with a pistol buckled on the outside. A broad yellow strip ran down the seams of his trousers; even his boots, spurs, and saddle were cavalry, indicating a recent discharge. He carried his right arm a bit stiffly, as though still pained by some serious wound.

The man shouted, "When are you going to fight the damned Indians? I've got to send something back to my paper."

"I'll let them come to me, Mr. Dandridge," McCracken said.

When the sutler's wagons approached,

he wheeled his horse away from Fields Dandridge and pulled in close to the lead team. The rumble of caisson wheels, the snap of harness, the wrenching creak of carriages warping to the irregular terrain was a din and that blocked out all sounds except those of the fife and drum. Somehow these came through, demanding to be heard.

McCracken leaned from the saddle to shout, "There's no change, Mike. What do you think they'll do?" McCracken was afraid the question made him sound incompetent. He wished that he could explain himself, make them understand that he was not one of those lock-jawed officers who kept their own counsel until the last shot was fired, just so they could write it up in their memoirs.

"By God, they'll fight! And I wish I'd stayed in Platte Station an' waited for the cavalry." Mike waved a hand toward the hills. "That's Chief Gall, boy, and it don't look good out there."

Mike Janis was a small man, prune-dried by the years in this graceless country. Yet his years here had blessed him with a keen knowledge and insight into the land and the savage Sioux. He was dry-skinned and dry-humored, and around his eyes and lips was a pinched, worried look. "Dang it all, a man ought'n to have such bad luck as to be escorted by horse artillery." He spat. "When I contracted to haul supplies and army brass, I expected cavalry to guard me. Why don't you dig in, boy? Ain't no sense in gettin' ambushed out in the open."

"I can't fight here," McCracken yelled. "Mike, I'll keep going as long as they stay out there."

"Guess that's all you can do," Janis admitted; he knew McCracken too. "I'd feel better, though, if your men was carryin' carbines instead of swabs."

McCracken smiled. He was tall and whippet-thin. His hair and mustache were red, nearly as red as the large neckerchief tied around his throat. He yelled, "In case they come at us, move straight ahead. You got that, Mike?"

"I got it," Janis said. He gave McCracken a glance full of warning. "Don't get cocky now, Bob. We got the colonel with us."

McCracken did not need the reminding. In the second wagon, Mike's daughter Marta handled the team as well as a man, and riding along in sullen discomfort were three officer's wives, foolishly joining their husbands at Fort Fetterman. McCracken figured that Marta Janis could handle herself as well as most men, but the army women were a bother. Each night tents had to be pitched and water carried for their baths. Mrs. Glendennon, the wife of Colonel Brubaker's aide, was no trouble at all, and McCracken suspected it was because her husband's junior rank left her on the fringe of unimportance. But the other two, both wives of field-grade officers, demanded drawing-room comfort and complained loudly when they didn't get it.

Turning his horse, McCracken rode back to the point, there relieving Lieutenant Borgnine, who returned to his own section. Through the day each man turned his flat-eyed attention toward the hills, and by the hour the enemy force swelled in numbers, drawn like ants to sweets by the ever-spiraling smoke signals. Worry was a common fester in the battery. McCracken had it, the one hundred and twenty-eight dollar a month kind, with fifteen more thrown in for command. The line privates had it too, but the army did not pay them much for theirs.

At the rest stop, Captain McCracken studied the Indian smoke through his field glasses. Lieutenant Borgnine was standing to one side with Lieutenants O'Fallon and Chaffee. When McCracken put away his glasses, Borgnine said, "I estimate over a hundred, sir."

"Well over," McCracken said quietly.

"If they mean to fight, why don't they come in?" O'Fallon asked. He had a smooth face common to the very young. A duck's down mustache tried valiantly to fill his upper lip.

Fields Dandridge came up on his fine horse and flung off. He stood spread-legged, beating dust from his clothes. His glance touched the junior officers, then passed on to McCracken. Dandridge was not a popular man, not because he was disagreeable but because he had enough money to keep five men for the rest of their lives. Fields Dandridge was not overweening about his wealth and McCracken had never heard him say that position was everything in life; but the officers resented his ability to spend the equivalent of their year's salary on a horse and never miss it. And McCracken knew they resented Dandridge's presence as correspondent for *Frank Leslie's Illustrated Weekly*. The opinion seemed to be that a man with a lot of money ought to keep his nose away from honest work.

"Is that Chief Gall?" Dandridge asked.

McCracken nodded, his gaze still on the hill.

"Mike Janis said he has a bullet in his leg that you put there six years ago when you were with Carrington." There was respect in Dandridge's voice and a shard of envy.

McCracken looked quickly at Dandridge, as though suspecting sarcasm behind the man's words. McCracken recalled the incident; he had always felt that he had come out second best, even though he had personally lamed the great chief. "That's right," McCracken said. "He's a bad Indian, Mr. Dandridge." He looked carefully at Dandridge. "You seem to be a man eager to continue your distinguished military career. Feel up to something? I can't spare an officer at this moment, and the job I have in mind I would hesitate to place in the hands of an enlisted man. So if you feel that you'd care to volunteer . . ."

"Yes, sir," Dandridge said. He almost clicked his heels.

McCracken took a pair of field glasses from his saddlebag and handed them to Fields Dandridge. "I want you to take these about a mile north of the column and place them on a rock where Gall can find them." He supposed that this gesture would be construed as bravado, something he hated in superior officers. Yet he felt that he should demonstrate some element of control and the glasses should do the trick. His name was plainly branded on the leather case and Gall would recognize his old foe.

"Sir?" Dandridge's voice was full of puzzlement.

"To my way of thinking," McCracken said, keeping his voice purposeful, "this waiting game is worse than a standstill fight. This present terrain suits me, but I need something to draw the Indians to me. I certainly can't chase them with artillery." McCracken's smile was wry. "Gall hates me too much to pass up a chance to get even." He said no more, feeling that he had already said enough.

An officer like the colonel, he thought, would have said nothing, feeling, of course, that junior officers don't need to understand a commander's purpose; their only function being to properly execute orders.

"Shall I display a white flag, sir?" Dandridge asked.

"You may not need it," McCracken said. "You've got a wonderful horse and I don't think they'll be able to hit you with their rifles."

"We'll soon see," Dandridge said as he vaulted into the saddle and stormed away.

Lieutenant O'Fallon said, "He's got more nerve than sense." His nervousness was excusable, since he was fresh to the army, a recent transplant from the Plain about the Hudson. His low marks at the Academy had left him with two miserable alternatives: infantry or artillery; and since he detested walking, he chose the latter. The once attractive prospect of combat grew less inviting as the probability increased to a now calculated certainty with McCracken's latest bit of madness. O'Fallon had heard rumors about Captain Robert Duward McCracken, and O'Fallon was inexperienced enough to have certain misgivings about his superior officer. If the talk ran correctly, there was bad blood between McCracken and Colonel Brubaker, who was now in the sutler's van. He had noticed that they scarcely spoke to each other. At one time, or so the story went, McCracken had mistaken, or ignored, a retreat order; and ended up holding the best piece of high ground the Confederates had, while Brubaker and his one thousand were idiotically entrenched a mile away. The subsequent necessity of explaining to the general staff embittered Brubaker and had started the mantle of 'jinx' which McCracken wore thereafter. It had also earned McCracken an implacable enemy in Colonel Brubaker.

Borgnine said, "I'd rather fight than have them dog-eye me another eighty miles." Borgnine's loyalty was of many years' duration, and McCracken silently thanked him for it.

"I'm ready," Wilson Chaffee said quickly. He pointed to a spot on the long slope. Dandridge had rid himself of the glasses and was now riding hell for leather, a whooping band of Sioux behind him, shooting as they pursued. Rifles snapped, but the shooting broke off when the Sioux found the field glasses. Dandridge came on in while the Sioux went back up the slope, whooping and flapping their arms.

Fields Dandridge flung himself off his blowing horse, then wiped away the sweat nettling his face. Chaffee said, "You could worry a man, Mr. Dandridge."

"I could worry myself," Dandridge admitted, grinning. "What a story to tell my children."

"If you live to have any," O'Fallon said. He stroked his mustache, which seemed reluctant to assume the proportions of McCracken's. "If Gall gets within rifle range, Captain, we're in trouble. The battery's spent so much time practicing maneuvers they've forgotten how to shoot a shoulder piece."

This was, McCracken supposed, the kind of criticism he could expect; his officers simply lacked faith in him. A sharp word here would be in order, but perhaps a casual word clarifying his intentions would be better. With this thought in mind, he said, "I have little intention of allowing my battery to revert to infantry, Mr. O'Fallon." He popped the lid of his hunting-case watch, glanced at it, and added, "Prepare to mount the column by section. Move on the drum, flank column."

"Section would be better," O'Fallon said. "Be less dust in single file."

McCracken frowned. Had Colonel Brubaker been commanding, he supposed that O'Fallon would be braced at attention and reamed out. He decided to say nothing and was glad of his

18

decision when Chaffee said, "For God's sake, Liam! You heard the order."

McCracken turned to his horse. He stepped into the saddle and waited until the section mounted. The artillerymen rode the draught horses, and on all the carriages and limbers. At McCracken's nod, the fife and drum gave the command to move, and once more the column moved along.

He did not call a halt until evening bivouac, nor did he glance back at his command. His attention was constantly on the hills and Chief Gall. There was little doubt in McCracken's mind now. Gall knew who the white invader was, and tomorrow could bring on a wave of Sioux thunder. McCracken's only comfort was that he had done everything he could to choose the time and place for the inevitable.

He selected open ground and gave his commands to the drummer. "First and second section — order in line to the left — MARCH."

Drivers hooted at the teams and

heavy caissons wheeled, breaking off from the column, turning out. While they were in motion, McCracken gave his second command. "Third and fourth sections — order in line to the right — MARCH."

The timing was the result of endless practice days. The drummer rolled, flammed, and rolled again and the command wheeled by sections, halting at one precise, unified moment. When the dust settled, the battery was in bivouac position, sections aligned back to back with the surprised Mike Janis and his wagons still between them. The supply wagon, under the command of the quartermaster sergeant, pulled up and sealed one end. McCracken's command post sealed the other end and he had his defense, his company street, his horse compound, with less fuss and bother than most infantry or cavalry commanders would have had.

Colonel Truman Brubaker dismounted from the sutler's van. He brushed at the dust clinging to his clothes then turned to his aide, Lieutenant Harry Glendennon. "I'll shave before evening mass."

"Yes, sir."

"And send Captain McCracken to my tent." He prepared a cigar for the match Glendennon hastily offered. He looked around at the packed battery. "A damn clumsy weapon, artillery. Glendennon, have you any idea what McCracken is up to?"

"No, sir," Glendennon said. He was a man touching thirty, darkly handsome. "May I suggest that you ask — "

Brubaker turned his head and stared at him. "Mr. Glendennon, I wouldn't ask Captain McCracken the time of day. The only reason I haven't taken command myself is I want to give him ample room to make his typically clumsy blunders." He struck his cigar into his mouth and puffed furiously.

"Well, sir, Captain McCracken's handling of the command — "

"Of course, of course," Brubaker

said, a bit impatiently. "But there's a marked difference between the drill field and a battle line."

"Yes, sir," Glendennon said. "Ah . . . if there's nothing else, I'd better fetch your shaving water and then see to my wife."

"Later," Brubaker said. He studied McCracken who stood near his command post. "Later, Mr. Glendennon. Right now I'm more interested in what Captain McCracken is going to do." He puffed on his cigar, letting the smoke dribble from his lips.

★ ★ ★

The sutler Mike Janis got down from his wagon, bending to remove the stiffness from his back. His daughter left the second wagon and joined him as McCracken came up. From the flanks, Fields Dandridge galloped in and flung off. He stood there, stripping off his gloves and waiting for someone to speak.

Mike Janis obliged. "Seen you give Gall them glasses. Consarned idiot. He'll take one look, recognize you, Bob, and come a-hellin'."

"That's why I sent them to him," McCracken said softly, a smile gently lifting his lips. "Thought you liked to fight, Mike."

"I fought Sioux all my life when I was with the Crows. But that Gall ain't no ordinary Injun, Bob. You ought to know that better'n the rest." He shook his head. "Seems to me there ought to be a safer way to make a living than hauling army supplies."

Marta Janis stirred, gently beating the dust from her clothes. She was a small girl, shapely, but not feminine in a pair of tight jeans and a man's faded shirt. Her hair was dark, as was her skin, gifts from a Crow mother. But her eyes were blue and steady. Fields Dandridge watched her. He had been watching her since he joined the train at Platte Station; and although he had spoken to her only a few times, there was no doubt in McCracken's mind about the way he felt.

Mike was worrying off a chew, and he spoke around it. "Brings to my mind another time when Gall whupped the army. He's smart and he's got the nerve of ten men. What you intend to do if he comes off that hill in the mornin', Bob?"

"Deploy and fight him," McCracken said. "That's what the army is out here to do, isn't it?"

Janis said. "Bob, I like you, but them boom guns of yours make a nervous wreck out of me. The gov'ment sent you out here to work out some newfangled tactics, didoes like you cut every night when we camp." He paused to spit. "Guess that'd be all right on a drill field, but this is war, Bob. And you got an all-fired mean Injun to do battle with. I got supplies to haul. If I don't get through, I'll lose my contract."

"Sir," Dandridge said, "can't you fire a round or two in their direction and scare them out of the hills?"

"When Gall comes off the hills in an attack," McCracken said, "I'll take your suggestion to heart, Mr. Dandridge."

"Hell," Janis said, "why wait?"

"Orders," McCracken said evenly. "I would like to get to Fort Fetterman before I open any new campaigns. But if I have to fight now, I want Gall to come to me on the terms as favorable to me as possible. That's been the reasoning behind everything I've done so far."

He thought of Colonel Truman Brubaker, waiting with silent patience, waiting for the mistake he was so sure would be made. That a field-grade officer could feel that way shook McCracken's confidence even further; he felt like a farm dog invited onto the parlor rug as a test of his manners, and he hated himself for feeling that way.

"Somebody better tell Gall that," Mike Janis said, and walked back to his wagon. He was typical of the civilians employed by the army; he distrusted their book-bound way of doing things, yet he criticized them for not giving more protection to his freight wagons. Still, Janis was an important link in the chain of frontier supply; the army would be helpless without him and his supply wagons.

Marta remained, and so did Fields Dandridge. McCracken said, "You can have supper in my tent if you like, Marta." He felt a strong bond with her, for in her way she regarded herself as an outcast. He recognized the error of her thinking much the same as he recognized his own sense of inferiority, yet the recognition didn't lessen the feeling.

She shook her head. "It would just start talk." For a moment he thought she was going to say more, but she was not one to talk much at any time. "I've got to help pa." With this she turned and started to walk away.

Fields Dandridge stared after her, then caught up in four strides. "I'll be glad to help you."

She stopped and looked at him. "Why?"

"Why?" He fumbled for an answer. "Because I'd like to."

"You don't owe me anything," Marta said. She turned on her heel and went to the second wagon and began fighting harness straps. Her father looked up from his work and saw Fields Dandridge standing where she had left him. Marta was shouldering the team around, Mike thought unhappily, as though she took pride in this lowly work. The job would have been difficult for a man; it was nearly impossible for her, but she managed to get the trace chains dropped.

McCracken observed this carefully, and was puzzled by Marta's action. He remembered her as being a friendly girl who laughed a lot. Dandridge turned away and went to his horse, leading him away. McCracken walked over to Mike Janis and said, "What's the matter with Marta?"

"She's a woman, that's what." He

looked at McCracken and knew that he didn't understand. "Half Injun, that's what's the matter." Janis moved past McCracken and spoke without looking around. "She was eleven when you left, Bob. A cute little girl who didn't think much about what her ma was. Now she's a woman and the color of her skin's against her. She knows it and it hurts like hell."

There was little McCracken could say. He walked over to where one of the corporals was erecting a tent for the field-grade officers' wives. He made a brief inspection and was cornered by Major Wyncoop's wife, who listed her daily accumulation of complaints in a shrill, authoritative voice. She was a prune-faced woman in her early forties who still longed to be thirty again. Sharp-tongued with junior officers, she was intolerable to enlisted men and second lieutenants. Neither O'Fallon nor Chaffee would get within hailing distance of her.

"Captain McCracken," she began, "I

fail to understand why an ambulance was not provided. I'll speak to the major about this when we reach Fetterman." She slapped her hands against her dress, booming away clouds of dust. "Living in filth like this . . . there'll be a report made. You can rely on it!"

"I'm sure I can," McCracken said, and the look she gave him protruded a good four inches from his back. He turned as Major Kisdeen's wife came from the wagon, puffing as though her bulk turned the slightest activity into work. She gave McCracken an icy smile. "What are you going to do about those Indians, Captain? They worry a body sick." She moved away, neither expecting an answer nor waiting for one.

McCracken walked on through the battery, inspecting. He could find no fault; the sections were ably commanded. But then, he had always believed that he commanded ably, which never quite seemed to be enough. Perhaps, he thought, I want too much. A man could break himself searching for a greatness that wasn't there; he had seen this happen to other men and the result was never pleasant.

He saw Colonel Brubaker's tent being pitched and walked toward it, drawn by the strict protocol that regulated his life. He saluted and had it halfheartedly returned; Brubaker did not bother to conceal his dislike.

"I'd like a report," Brubaker said. His cigar was a sour stub and he shied it away. "What are the damned Indians up to?" He glanced at McCracken, then went on as though he hadn't really expected an answer worth listening to. "Are you trying to pick a fight, Captain?"

"I would rather pick it, sir, on my own ground, than have one pressed on me while occupying difficult terrain."

"That's a hell of an answer," Brubaker said. "Carry on, Captain. But remember that this is not the drill field. What you do here goes on the record."

"I understand," McCracken said,

and walked quickly away. He went on to the column's head where his command post had been sent up. A tent had been pitched, a collapsible bunk and camp stools erected. The flap was open and he ducked his head as he entered.

Lieutenant Glendennon's wife was sitting on one of the stools, her bare feet in a bucket of water. She hastily lowered her skirts until they covered all but the calves of her legs. "I'm always outranked on the water bucket, Captain. I hope you don't mind the invasion."

McCracken did not know what to say; he certainly had no intention of being impolite, yet he felt uneasy about this woman. She had a husband who seemed determined to ignore her. But a husband had certain legal rights, and McCracken did not want Lieutenant Glendennon to get the impression they were being usurped; he had enough troubles without inviting more.

Sheila Glendennon was a woman

men noticed. She was tall and shapely and always poised. Her hair was very dark, her glance direct and appraising, like a commander viewing a new recruit to his officer staff for the first time.

McCracken took off his hat and pistol belt, tossing them on the bunk. "My orderly will be here soon with supper," he said. "Would you prefer to have yours here?"

"Thank you, it would be a welcome relief."

He didn't ask her from what. He didn't need to. Sheila Glendennon was not a woman who endeared herself to her own sex. With a certain amazement, McCracken realized that women understood those best who were full of small deceits, and suspected most strongly any woman who spoke and acted with frankness.

Darkness was coming on fast. He lighted a lantern and hung it on the tent pole. Sheila Glendennon removed her feet from the bucket and began to dry them. She crossed one leg over the

32

other, exposing part of her thigh, and McCracken obligingly turned his back until she slipped into her shoes. She smiled at this show of propriety but seemed pleased by it, too.

Sergeant Karopsik brought the meal. McCracken said, "Fetch another service for Mrs. Glendennon, Sergeant." Karopsik left, returning a moment later with another plate and cup. He set everything on the folding table and left. McCracken was content to eat and let the conversation slide for a while. And Sheila Glendennon knew enough about men to play along.

When he reached for his coffee, she said, "There seems to be a split opinion about what you should do with the Indians, Captain."

"Yes," he admitted. "Which side is your husband on?"

"Harry?" She laughed. "he believes whatever the colonel tells him to believe. Did you really leave a pair of glasses for Chief Gall? I think that's very daring, Captain. Harry would never have been so rash."

"I didn't do it to be rash," he said. "Gall and I are old enemies. It started a few years back when I went to Kearney with Carrington and his hopeless expedition. Gall was a bad one and we had many a fight. Once I left a bullet in his leg, which he still carries, and it makes him limp badly."

"Oh," she said. "Are you renewing a feud with Colonel Brubaker, too? He doesn't like you."

"Perhaps he has his reasons," he said. "Is this your first trip to the frontier?" He felt a strong need to swing the conversation away from himself; she was quite expert at prying and still managing to sound innocent.

"Yes. Harry thought I might like it. Do you agree, Captain? Is it as exciting as the newspapers lead you to believe?"

"Well, I've always had my duty, which has left me without much leisure. Mike Janis could tell you anything you want to know."

"I'd rather have you tell me," she said. "Those artillery pieces are French, aren't they?"

He felt relieved at the sudden switch to another topic. "The very latest," he said. "The French are far ahead of us in fieldpieces. You know, since the Rebellion, artillery has almost been done away with in the army. I hope to revive it as a first-line arm."

"Very ambitious," Sheila said. "But I understand that you've always been ambitious. Now Harry — that's my husband — is not ambitious at all. We quarrel about it quite often."

"There's no need to tell me," he said. McCracken had a distinct dislike for secrets. He supposed this was because he was himself too shy to take others into his confidence. Secrets entailed a certain obligation and he wanted no more than a casual relationship with Mrs. Glendennon; he could not bring himself to think of her as Sheila.

"I wanted to," she said. "When two people are not happy with each other, I see no need to hide it." She leaned forward. "Captain, aren't you bothered by what other people think about you?"

The bluntness of her question shocked him momentarily, then his own honesty made him admit that this shock came from an inability to talk away his real problems. For many years he had listened to other officers frankly discussing their anger and the pain of slights or misfortunes, and he had envied them. But all he could do was pretend that he was too thick-skinned to care. "I have other things to occupy me," he said, somewhat stiffly. "It's my hope to write the artillery manual for the army. I've worked out a completely new set of maneuvers for horse artillery." He shrugged. "Perhaps I'm the fool they all label me. Washington brass think I'm crazy. They even sent Fields Dandridge along to take down my failure, incident by incident. But I really don't give a damn about their collected opinions. I have eight French guns and General Philip St. George Cooke's reluctant approval to reinforce Fort Runyon."

He finished his coffee and set the cup aside. "I understand that Colonel Brubaker, who is soon to be the new commandant of Fort Fetterman, expected a troop of cavalry. Likely he'll never get over the shock of getting me, with a battery of horse artillery."

"Do you really think the army can activate Fort Runyon with Gall on the rampage?" Sheila asked. "I'm interested because Harry is being sent there as soon as the . . . ah . . . cavalry arrive." She nodded toward the vastness outside the tent. "If Gall turns you back now, the colonel will consider that a failure of your tactics. I think he would enjoy reporting that you failed."

Robert McCracken smiled. "Mrs. Glendennon, I don't think Gall can turn me back."

"Ah, determined as well as ambitious." She stood up. "Thank you for a most pleasant hour, but now I have to get back. Tongues, you know, and a suspicious if indifferent husband."

"I'll walk with you."

"I'd have been hurt if you hadn't offered," she said, and went out with him. Squad fires burned in bright rows and around them artillerymen lounged and talked softly, taking a brief ease from hard duty. Guards circled the horse herds and the night was quiet. He said good night by Mrs. Glendennon's wagon and started back, cutting through Mike Janis's camp. As he approached the colonel's wagon he saw an irregular shape by the tailgate but thought nothing of it until it moved. Then he stopped, unflapped his pistol holster and curled his fingers around the butt.

"Who goes there?" When he stepped close, Lieutenant Harry Glendennon pressed back against the tailgate where the shadows were ink.

"Step out here," McCracken said softly. "What are you hiding for?"

"This is my wagon," Glendennon

said. "I'm not hiding." There was a native belligerence about him that he did not bother to conceal. He stood spraddle-legged, his gloves tucked into his belt.

"I'm not going to argue the point with you," McCracken said. "If you have something on your mind, then get it off."

"The next time you invite my wife to supper, ask me first." For a time he remained silent and McCracken waited. Finally, Glendennon said, "I was going to come to your tent but I changed my mind. I don't like to settle unpleasant business in front of my wife."

"What do you find unpleasant about it?" McCracken asked. He took Glendennon's arm and turned him so the faint night light fell on the harsh angles of his face. "I asked you a question, Mister!"

"Stay away from my wife," Glendennon said.

For a moment McCracken stood in

39

stunned silence. He tried to understand this man, who was obviously not blind. "Mr. Glendennon, in order to grant that request it will be necessary for you to keep her out of my tent."

"What kind of a lie is this?"

"Mr. Glendennon," McCracken said, his voice like broken glass, "I would consider a moment before I called anyone a liar. This isn't a matter of pulling rank. If you want to carry this further, let's go outside the picket line where we'll have privacy to settle this."

This was a long speech for McCracken and he waited to see what effect it would have.

Finally, Lieutenant Glendennon wheeled abruptly and went around the far side of the wagon. McCracken walked on, soon passing out of sight.

Glendennon paused before Colonel Brubaker's tent. The colonel came out, a cigar clamped between his teeth. "Quarreling with McCracken over your wife?" Brubaker asked.

"He was ready to fight about it," Glendennon said. "Sir, I don't want my wife going to him."

"Stop acting like a jealous husband," Brubaker said. "She doesn't mean that much to you and you know it."

"Just the same, sir — "

"Mr. Glendennon," Brubaker said, "I must confess that I suggested to your wife that she go to Captain McCracken's tent. She came to me and complained about the water; the other ladies seem to use it all up before she gets a chance to wash." He smiled faintly. "I've observed you two together, and I know you don't get along, so I fail to see the root of your jealousy." He paused a moment. "Mr. Glendennon, let me put it another way: which is more important to you? Making captain or holding onto a wife you don't get along with?"

"I — I don't believe I know what you mean, sir?"

"It isn't necessary for you to know," Brubaker said. "Suppose we allow events to pursue a natural course."

"Between Sheila and McCracken?"

"Yes," Brubaker said. "Isn't that worth a captain's bars?" He patted Glendennon on the arm. "You're an intelligent man, Mr. Glendennon. Intelligent enough to see the advantages of pleasing your commanding officer."

"Yes, sir."

After Glendennon walked away, Colonel Brubaker stood in the shadows, enjoying his cigar and considering the risks he was running just to even an old score. He felt that he could play Glendennon without revealing anything incriminating; after all, the man was a junior officer and ambitious enough to do what he was told.

And Sheila Glendennon was just pretty enough, and disgusted enough with her husband, to find another man attractive. Brubaker smiled. A good officer always considered every means of defeating his opponent, and Brubaker decided that scandal was as effective as field tactics.

He decided that he had told Glendennon just enough to arouse his ambitious loyalty, yet not enough to speak of it later so that blame could be laid at his feet. Glendennon might guess that Brubaker was out to get Robert McCracken, but he would never be able to prove it.

★ ★ ★

Sergeant Fydor Karopsik was waiting in McCracken's tent when he stepped inside. The sergeant came to instant attention. "Shall I double the guard tonight, sir?" He was one of those old-school, continental soldiers who maintained a mummy-stiffness when addressing an officer.

"No," McCracken said, stripping off his blouse and boots. From a bucket he poured water into a pewter wash basin and sloshed his face. "I've never heard of a Plains Indian who liked to attack at night, Sergeant. So we'll take

43

advantage of that. Wake me at one o'clock."

"Yes, sir," Karopsik said and went out immediately.

After blowing out the lantern, Robert Duward McCracken undressed. He shifted about, trying to find a nonexistent comfort on the army cot. His first consideration now was getting his command through, and that could be a knotty problem with Gall waiting with animal patience to kill off another segment of the hated army. And after he got through, there would be Colonel Brubaker, who hated the artillery as well as the man who commanded it.

At one o'clock, Sergeant Karopsik's touch brought McCracken to instant wakefulness. "Time, sir," the sergeant said.

"Thank you," McCracken said, sitting up. He rubbed his eyes. "Wake Lieutenants Borgnine and Chaffee, Sergeant. Have them report here quietly."

"Yes, sir."

McCracken sat on the edge of his cot and reconsidered his earlier decision to draw Chief Gall into a fight. Bit by bit, he took his plan apart, examined each piece, then reassembled it, like an apprentice watchmaker learning his craft. He could find no apparent flaw, but this did not lull him into any false sense of security. Other plans had looked good only to come unraveled under the press of action. He stopped and considered the possibility that his entire concept of artillery tactics might be wrong; if they were, many men would soon die to prove it. McCracken sighed. Again he was moving close to the brink of disgrace; a good defeat could see him summarily dismissed, with not even half pay.

The thought brought beads of sweat to his forehead but he stuck to his determination not to turn back.

McCracken dressed in the dark, then lighted the lantern when he heard the two officers approaching. His attention sharpened as his ears picked up a third step and Fields Dandridge entered with the others.

"Do you mind, sir? I couldn't sleep."

"No, it's all right," McCracken said. He waved the two officers onto the cot and they waited. "Gentlemen, I think we're in for a real fight if we wait until morning to move off this high plateau." He brought out a map and indicated their present position. "The road to the south cuts away from this high ground. For days now we've been gradually reaching the higher terrain." He pointed to a spot on the west side. "Here the ground slopes sharply. The pass down is here. We'll be exceedingly vulnerable once we enter that two-mile stretch."

"What do you suggest?" Borgnine asked.

"I think you'd better assume command here," McCracken said. "Mr. Chaffee and I will take two pieces from the first section and move ahead tonight, quietly. We'll leave the limbers behind. There's sufficient ammunition on the gun carriages for our purpose."

"Can we get off at night, sir?" Chaffee asked this.

"I think it's a matter of our needing to get off," McCracken said. "Prepare two gun squads for moving, Mr. Chaffee."

"Very well, sir." Chaffee beat a retreat. Borgnine and Dandridge remained.

"This sounds risky," Borgnine said. "An unfamiliar trail at night, sir."

"The risks are part of the game," McCracken said. "Carry on, Mr. Borgnine, and we'll try to effect a quiet withdrawal so as not to alarm the Indians camped in the hills above us."

After Borgnine left, Dandridge said, "What are our chances, sir?"

"I can't accurately measure them," McCracken said. He smiled. "You're not a man who worries about chances, are you, Mr. Dandridge?"

"No, sir. I'd like to go along with you and Lieutenant Chaffee."

"All right," McCracken said.

After Dandridge left, McCracken put on his gloves and hat and went through the area toward Mike Janis's wagons. He found the man snoring and woke him.

"What you want, Bob?" He pawed at his whiskered face and smacked his lips loudly.

"How well do you know this terrain?"

"Like the back of my hand."

"I'll need you," McCracken said. "And I'll need Marta to guide the command off this high ground in the morning."

"You figurin' to move out tonight?"

He considered taking Mike Janis into his confidence; the man was an old friend and could be trusted. Yet McCracken hesitated. The fact that he intended to sneak part of the battery off the high ground and bait a trap for Gall was really a commander's business, so he kept his answer short. "A part of the battery. Is Marta in her wagon?"

"She'd better be," Janis said.

McCracken touched him on the shoulder and walked to the rear of Marta's wagon. He could see her vaguely, blanket to her chin. He touched her lightly and felt her jump, instantly awake. The muzzle of a .44 poked out at him and he brushed it aside. "Are you dressed?"

"I've got some clothes on," she admitted.

"Then dress and come with me," he said. He waited a few minutes, then she stepped from the wagon, her pistol belt over one shoulder. McCracken walked with her to his tent. The first and second squads' gun carriages were being limbered and Borgnine had thoughtfully muzzled the clanking trace chains in blankets.

"What's going on?" Marta asked.

"We're going to try to get down the west slope without a lot of noise," he told her.

"The whole shebang?"

"Just two guns and twelve horses."

"Why?" she asked.

49

Borgnine's arrival cut off his explanation. "All ready, sir."

"Fine. If there are any spare blankets, have the quartermaster stow them in the two carriages."

Borgnine left and Marta Janis said, "Bob, you'd be smarter if you dug in here and let them come to you."

"We're not infantry," he said, and went outside, Marta following him. "Getting down in broad daylight to the flats will set this battery up like a country fair turkey shoot," McCracken said. "So I'm going to take two guns off tonight and dig in. When Gall tries to catch us, I'll have a surprise waiting for him."

"What do you want with me?"

"Your father's going with me," he said. "I want you to lead Borgnine and the rest of the command off at dawn. You know the trail, don't you?"

"Blindfolded," She jerked her thumb toward Brubaker's tent. "You going to let jelly-belly in on this scheme?"

"No," McCracken said.

There was a slight delay while the quartermaster brought up the blankets, then McCracken's orderly arrived with the horses, already saddled.

Mike Janis appeared, one cheek full of tobacco. He saw that they were all mounted and stepped into the saddle, moving on McCracken's signal.

There wasn't much of a moon, just enough to break the bony blackness. The rise was thickly grassed and the carriage wheels were muffled by it. A mile from the night bivouac, McCracken halted to have the carriage wheels wrapped in blankets. A short march later they came to a wash leading down to the flats, a steeply pitched drop-off cluttered by bucket-sized rocks.

At McCracken's direction, a detail walked ahead, clearing these rocks out of the way. The darkness made slow work of everything and at times the carriages threatened to overrun the teams. Two hours of sweat-raising labor brought them to the flats. McCracken looked at the sky and judged the dawn to be an hour away.

Summoning Lieutenant Wilson Chaffee, McCracken gave his orders. "Take your squad over there at least three hundred yards." He pointed to the right of the trail. "Do not dig in, and have the horse holders keep the team in harness ready for instant unlimbering."

"Yes, sir."

"Remember, Mr. Chaffee, the most dangerous moment for artillery is the moment of unlimbering. In that position you can neither fight nor run.

"Will that be all, sir?" Chaffee asked.

"No. Your field of fire will be mutually supporting with mine. You will fire to the left so that it crosses mine. Get on with it now."

When Chaffee wheeled his horse, Dandridge said, "Can I go along with his section, Captain?"

"By all means," McCracken said. His attention then turned to his own squad and the positioning of the single gun. He chose a post three hundred yards to the left of the trail, thereby separating the artillery pieces by six hundred yards. The range where the fire crossed was five hundred yards ahead, point-blank range; and a good gunner could knock a horse down with the first shot at that distance.

McCracken left his own gun limbered, that is, harnessed, trails up, ready to move. The men exchanged glances and recalled the hours on the drill ground. This time unlimbering would be 'for the record', because by waiting until the enemy actually appeared, McCracken duplicated a situation of surprise which was often fatal to artillery when caught in battle by a troop of cavalry.

Mike Janis was waiting to one side, watching the sky to the east, waiting for the first blush of the false dawn. Finally he said, "You ought to be blockin' the trail down. You've got a big gap there and they'll come right straight through."

"That remains to be seen," McCracken said.

Sergeant Max Heinzman, who was McCracken's gunner, came up with the sighting telescope. He extended the tripod legs, plumbed the instrument level, then stepped back so McCracken could peer through it. He spoke without taking his attention from the eyepiece. "When you get the command to unlimber, Sergeant, the range will be five-eight-zero. I suspect that they'll come in from that slight depression out there, having circled us effectively. There's enough drop to the land to mask their movements."

The dawn was fully awakened now and in a few short moments, shards of sunlight were cutting across the land. Through the signalman, McCracken relayed the range and elevation to Chaffee. Heinzman was waiting beside his gun. McCracken was looking at the ground, gouging it with his boot heel. "Spongy," he said softly, talking to himself. "Sergeant, a round of explosive, please. The ground is soft and the projectile will implant. No chance of a ricochet."

A round was pushed into the hastily opened breech and followed with a bag of powder and detonating charge. Chaffee's crew was alert and waiting. Every man gazed level at the breast of the slope.

Heinzman said, "Sir, with this elevation, I figure our fire will fall short by thirty yards."

McCracken smiled. "Sergeant, we're not going to slaughter them unless it's necessary. A round in front of them may do more to discourage them than a round in their midst."

"Yes, sir." Heinzman seemed satisfied.

Mike Janis wasn't. "My dead wife's people fought the Sioux before the white man ever came out here," he said. "You'll never scare Gall off, Bob. You ought to know that."

"Gall's only one man," McCracken said. "If his command discipline breaks, he can't hope to attack alone."

55

Janis made a snorting noise in his throat and checked the loads in his pistol.

McCracken watched him and said, "You won't need that, Mike."

"Just in case," he said. "Bob, Gall's going to ride right up and spit in your eye." He slid the .44 back into the holster and squatted, his legs crossed. "As far as he's concerned, you'd be better off if you killed him the first shot."

McCracken took off his hat and found sweat on his forehead, although the morning heat was not that strong. His eyes never left that rise of land and while he watched, the sun climbed higher, trailing a thin heat.

The need to explain anything was gone now, the newest private had figured it out for himself. McCracken was in position with two fieldpieces and he hoped to hold Gall back when the Indian chief chose to attack the main battery coming off the hill. Waiting for anything had never been easy for

McCracken. When a boy, he had been impatient to be a man; and once that stature had been attained, he looked on to new horizons. By nature he was impulsive. He proved that when he was twelve, leaving his home in Glasgow for the uncertain world of America.

He began to consult his watch and by degrees the morning marched toward noon. On the rise of land only the wind-ruffled grass moved and he wondered if his luck would hold and Chief Gall would fall for the trap. Would he wait to attack until the column started off the high ground in hopes that he would catch them helpless as they fought the slope?

That the Indian might have outguessed him was a strangling pill for McCracken to swallow, yet he was accustomed to failure. His carefully prepared position could be his greatest handicap, because if Gall chose to split his forces and attack sooner, McCracken would be unable to make more than a token fight. Gall would be able to charge clean through and McCracken would have to give up his hope of stopping him. Thin his ranks he might, but stop him, no.

McCracken figured that the battery would start down off the hill around ten o'clock, and as that time neared his nervousness increased. A man worked, thought, applied himself, but he could only go so far on paper. There came a time when each theory had to be tested in the field, and now that his own moment was drawing near, he could not recall ever having felt so completely isolated and alone.

His decisions to this point were like a chain, and in the space of minutes he would find out its strength and weaknesses. Robert Duward McCracken, Captain, 7th Light Artillery, was about to rise from the obscurity of the military treadmill, or sink into it beyond recovery.

Mike Janis interrupted his thoughts, "Bob, you'd better change your order and fire into that flock."

"The order stands," he said.

"Captain!"

Heinzman's voice brought McCracken's eyes to the horizon. He drew in his breath sharply and held it, stunned by the sight of two hundred warriors in a line abreast.

"Unlimber!" he shouted, and the signalman relayed the order to Chaffee, whose crew went into immediate action. The Indians saw the guns being readied and began to surge into motion. A drumming filled the air as they came on, breaking into a ragged run. The artillerymen were straining at the trails, dropping them, and the sound building in their ears was an excellent goad for speed.

On the hill behind McCracken, the rumble of carriage wheels added to the sounds. Borgnine was starting down. The Sioux came on, closing the distance, poised like a spear for the death-thrust, their numbers overwhelming.

McCracken was in control of himself

now. "Sergeant, a round of explosives."
His tension, his doubts had suddenly
vanished.

Fourteen years in the Imperial German
Army gave Sergeant Heinzman a certain
polish, a special touch. He yanked the
lanyard; the fieldpiece roared, driving
back against the steel rails, rearing,
wheels momentarily off the ground.
The sudden detonation was a bursting
pain inside the skull, and Mike Janis
clapped his hands over his ears.

The Sioux broke off their charge,
milling when a geyser of earth erupted
before them, throwing part of their
line into panic. Horses reared, spilling
riders. Others turned, running into the
braves arrayed behind them. But some
of the Sioux rallied and fired irregular
volleys at McCracken's crew. A soldier
near Heinzman whipped around, then
began to vomit blood while another
stared stupidly at a bullet-shattered
arm. All around them McCracken saw
small bombs of earth, as though a mild,
invisible hailstorm were descending,

then he realized that these were Sioux bullets.

Lieutenant Chaffee's gun spoke with a dull boom and another tall spout of earth shot upward. Chaffee's elevation had been correct, but a portion of the charging Indians ran into the burst, leaving a gap of downed and dying. The rank stayed open, the vacancies like missing teeth in a grinning boy's mouth.

The Indians tried to rally to Gall, who shouted and waved his rifle, but there was too much disorganization for him to regroup.

"Another round, Sergeant," McCracken said.

Heinzman's squad was well drilled. Before the blown earth had settled from Chaffee's shot, he had his piece reloaded. He pulled the lanyard and instantly Chaffee's shot echoed the boom. Two more towers of earth flew up, scant seconds apart. The cries of terrorized Indians came clearly across the distance, and in a mass of panic they wheeled and disappeared from sight.

McCracken looked at Mike Janis, who just stared, still stunned by the effect of the artillery. "Swab bores, Sergeant. Then reload," McCracken said.

"Aye, sir!"

He forced himself to take a look at the damage. Somehow he never had the stomach to look at a soldier who had been killed carrying out his orders, but he did look. One dead, one wounded, and Heinzman was tending to him. Two of the horses were down and shrieking; they were shot immediately. Through the sighting telescope McCracken could see Chaffee's squad, three men thinner now.

Mike patted his ears to still the loud ringing. "This isn't over yet, Bob. Gall was scared off, but he'll be back."

"And we'll try to be ready for him," McCracken said. "Go on up the hill and help your girl get the others off."

Mike turned to his horse and mounted, riding up the slope where Lieutenant Borgnine and Marta Janis were laboring the column down.

A half-hour later the command formed on the flats. Borgnine rode up, grinning. "Sir, I never saw anything like it. My squad would have given a month's pay to have been behind those pieces."

"Well," McCracken said, "certain optimists among us feel that they'll be back." His voice was calm, but he knew it was camouflage for the uneasiness he felt inside.

Mounting his own horse, McCracken rode toward the sutler's wagons. He passed the grinning Mike Janis and went on to the third wagon in which the officer's ladies rode. They waved and smiled, pleased that he had at last exhibited some usefulness. When he passed Brubaker in the sutler's van, he touched his fingers to the brim of his hat, unwilling to stop and listen to the colonel's blistering criticism of the fight; he would hear that officially when they reached Fetterman.

To any man in the command the action had been a success, but a written report could change that easily. McCracken was familiar with those reports, their content and purpose. The tactics had been untried, and to many old-line soldiers, basically unsound. That he had succeeded would seem like pure idiot's luck, when properly told, and Brubaker was just the man to tell it that way.

With a touch of guilt, McCracken recalled his own use of a written report. At the time he had felt fully justified but now he was no longer sure. The man had been a brevet major named Davis — drunk on duty. McCracken had painted a rather ugly picture, and it seemed even uglier when he learned that Davis had been permanently frozen in rank, a heavy stigma for a military man to carry . . .

He found Mrs. Glendennon walking and slid from the saddle to walk beside her. He knew this was unwise, yet he felt unaccountably comfortably with her, completely free from military concern. Dust limed her face and clothes and perspiration had soaked her dress under the arms and across the shoulders, yet she dredged up a smile for him.

"You're quite a hero," she said.

"Not too heroic," he said. "I fought from a stationary position with every advantage on my side." He knew Brubaker would make a point of this.

"Who cares? You stopped Chief Gall." She frowned slightly. "Or are you concerned only with your military tactics?"

"I'm concerned with proving they are superior." Then he smiled. "I was scared out there. Did you know that?"

"I was hoping you were," she said, smiling. "I like a man who's human enough to be scared when he has sufficient reason. And honest enough to admit it."

He left her then, returning to the

point where he set the column in march order. There was much about the Sioux, and Chief Gall in particular, that Captain McCracken could admire, especially their courage. While his command gathered, chosen warriors rode into view to gather the dead. McCracken sat his horse and watched them parade boldly, rifles waving in defiance to the white invader.

There were his dead to bury, and McCracken forced his weak stomach under control and walked over to where they lay. He saw Private Jenkin's wide, sightless eyes, and felt a little ashamed that he knew so little about the man. Nothing, really. Nothing save Jenkin's ability to clamp the rim of a quart beer bucket between his teeth and drink it, no hands, without a pause for breath. Corporal Allen lay face down; someone had kindly turned him that way because Allen now had no face.

Motioning for Lieutenant Chaffee to come up, McCracken said, "See that a burying detail is formed. We'll take an hour."

McCracken stood alone while the graves were dug and the dead men placed in blankets. Then he took a worn prayer book from his saddle bag and read briefly. Borgnine was ready to move out; McCracken spoke to the drummer. "Flank column. Give the roll at will."

The march began again and sounds clashed with deeper sounds, becoming a din. Dust rose thick and choking. Dull monotony commenced anew. This was, McCracken knew, the way of all war; a small island of action surrounded by an ocean of monotony.

Fields Dandridge sided him, a wide smile splitting his young face. "I really have something to send back to the paper!"

"Such as?" McCracken asked.

"Why, the battle," Dandridge said.

"I think that the battle hasn't yet begun," McCracken said slowly.

Through the afternoon's pushing

sunlight, they moved northwest. Mike Janis came up to ride on McCracken's right, strangely silent, and he made no overture to break his silence. With each mile traveled, the country became more open; and without the small rises of land to conceal the flanks, he saw that the Sioux were paralleling his march line. The command moved at a walk, and the solid line of warriors paced him but stayed well out, over a thousand yards.

This watching game went on for an hour; the artillery still maintaining a parade walk, the enemy flanking at the same speed. McCracken was a soldier and he saw the shrewd purpose behind Gall's thinking. Two solid lines of enemy strength gave the Sioux a tremendous advantage should they choose to turn and charge straight on. And from all appearances, they were considering that.

Mentally, McCracken made a few calculations, estimating the time it would take the hostiles to cover eight hundred of the thousand yards; they would have to get in that close to use their rifles. He also estimated the time it would take to unlimber and fight.

But Gall was too strong for him to fight here. He turned in the saddle and waved Lieutenant Gustave Borgnine forward. "Mr. Borgnine," he said, "inform the section chiefs that we're going to make a night march into Fetterman."

"Yes, sir," Borgnine said, and wheeled back through the column.

He tried not to think of Brubaker's discomfort; he knew he would hear about that, too, when they reached Fetterman. Probably would go into his record. And a man's record could only stand so much.

Returning his attention to the Indians, McCracken realized that they were slowly moving in, narrowing the margin of safety. At four o'clock the Sioux were a mere six hundred yards out. McCracken again signaled Borgnine forward. "By my estimate," he said, "the Indians will be able to cover approximately two hundred yards before a squad can wheel out, unlimber into battery, and prepare to fire. When the hostiles approach to within five hundred yards, I will signal you to fall out of the column, one squad at a time. Unlimber, and go into battery facing the left flank. Load and lock, Mr. Borgnine. But if it becomes necessary to fire, direct your fire ahead of them, not into them."

"Yes, sir," Borgnine said, but if he had had his own way he'd have fired a round into them; his expression said so.

"When the other sections pass you," McCracken said, "limber and fall in again. Another squad will then go into position. You understand, Gus. We've drilled on this maneuver."

"I understand," Borgnine said, and rode back. He signaled his section to readiness and passed it back to Chaffee and O'Fallon.

Mike Janis said, "Ain't you going to stop the column to fight?"

70

"I'll have a squad in battery at all times," he said. "We'll proceed at a parade walk." His glance went to the Indians and he saw that they were even closer than before, yet he felt strangely calm.

McCracken did not look back at Colonel Brubaker; he could feel the constant pressure of the man's eyes, watching and judging. Since leaving Platte Station, Brubaker had remained aloof, like a judge trying a very important case. McCracken had politely offered Brubaker the command, this was a common courtesy to superior officers, but Brubaker had declined.

And not without reason, McCracken thought grimly. He wants me to be completely responsible. If I make enough little mistakes, he'll write them in his report and finish me. If I make a big one, he'll relieve me of my command on the spot and I'll have to resign my commission.

Either way, he stood to lose everything and gain little.

Mike Janis raised his hand and wiped moisture from his face. "Bob, don't you have enough sense to be scared? Why don't you open up? Afraid you'll miss?"

"I could hit them at eight times this distance," McCracken said and turned away. Fields Dandridge rode up and joined them. He looked out at the hostiles and said, "Whatever I said about the fight we had before, forget it. I think this time we're in for a real one."

"When it starts," McCracken said, "I want you to ride back and take care of Mike's daughter."

"Sure," Dandridge said.

"She can take care of herself," Mike snapped, then looked at Fields Dandridge and closed his mouth. "All right. I won't argue about it."

McCracken watched Gall, who crept slowly closer. When he judged the distance to be his present minimum, he turned and said, "Mr. Borgnine!"

Immediately Borgnine's squad wheeled.

72

Artillery men jumped off the carriage before it stopped. Trace chains were flung off, and the team led to one side and held there in harness. The limber was detached from the trails and the gun dropped to cover the left flank. The gunners stood ready while the company marched slowly by. When the last limber passed, the horses were rehitched, the limber recoupled and the section wheeled in column to the rear. A section on the right flank had dropped out and was going into battery.

Watching both his men and the enemy, McCracken felt like a man walking the tightest of wires. For two miles this falling out and falling in went on, and the strain of the labor was beginning to tell on the soldiers. McCracken knew this maneuver was for short duration and not for a prolonged, running fight. A battery might possibly keep this up for an hour, or an hour and a half at the most, but in the end they would have to take a stationary position of defense.

Long shadows of evening began to flatten ahead of the column and McCracken saw, with some satisfaction, that his maneuvering had held the Sioux back. The black maws of the three pounders were too impressive a threat to ignore, especially since Gall had already received one wicked taste.

War, McCracken knew, was essentially a dangerous game of bluff. He was aware that a simultaneous charge by both flanks would necessitate a complete halt, and in the end he would be overpowered by sheer numbers. He was defending himself on threat alone. Gall knew and yet he hesitated, worrying about how many of his warriors would die while they covered that five-hundred-yard interval.

And as long as they worried, they kept their distance.

Late afternoon shadows turned to the first smudge of evening, then suddenly the Sioux gave up. With one long cry they wheeled and rode away, leaving

Captain Robert McCracken weak with relief.

At his signal, the section now in battery limbered up for the last time, falling in at the tail of the column.

Fields Dandridge came up and said, "I'm ten years older, Captain. Do you do this sort of thing often?"

"Alternate Tuesdays," McCracken said.

"Tuesday could be my bad day," Dandridge said, wheeling his horse.

Colonel Truman Brubaker sent Lieutenant Glendennon forward to fetch McCracken to the sutler's van. The colonel was perched on the high seat like a fat crow eyeing a cornfield. When McCracken sided him, Brubaker took the cigar from his mouth and said, "You were lucky. I hope you know that."

"I think it more than luck, sir."

Brubaker smiled, his rotund face wrinkling. "Do you, now? Captain, it is my opinion that the Indians chose to leave of their own free will. I am not convinced that your artillery frightened them."

"They left," McCracken said, "because they wanted no more taste of artillery."

"Your assumption is fantastic," Brubaker said. "Captain, you lost some men at the foot of the pass. Only a miracle kept them from annihilating you." He put his cigar between his lips and rolled it to the corner of his mouth. "You've had two strokes of exceptional luck, Captain. I prophesy that it will run out shortly after we reach Fetterman, and my reports are telegraphed East."

McCracken touched fingers to his cap. "I've no doubt of that, sir. Now, if you'll excuse me . . . " He spurred his horse forward to the head of the column.

2

ASENTRY first saw the dust column in the early morning and made his report to the corporal of the guard, who, in turn, summoned the officer of the day from his game of horseshoes behind the regimental stables. Lieutenant Lydecker was the duty officer, a tall persimmon of a man whose credo consisted of smiling only for superior officers and shouting at all lesser ranks. He came onto the palisade ramp, studied the dust through his field glasses, then descended to strut across the parade. He entered the commanding officer's spare quarters and woke him from a sound nap.

Brevet Colonel Clifton Ellis grumbled at Lydecker, who stood stiffly while the colonel stomped into his boots and hooked his saber into the frog.

"The new commanding officer, Mr. Lydecker?" Ellis's face was florid from the early morning heat and the sudden awakening left him in a peckish humor. The colonel's hair was nearly white, and according to him, this had been brought about by twenty-eight years of commanding nothing but idiots. His enormous mustache had not known a razor's edge for years.

"I believe so, sir," Lydecker said. "And from the dust raised, it must be a regiment."

"Nonsense," Ellis said and stomped out, his boots raising puffs of dust as he crossed the parade, Lydecker at his heels. Colonel Ellis walked with the waddle of the overweight. He had an infantryman's big feet and he planted them solidly with each step. He climbed the ladder to the ramp and when he reached the wall, puffed for wind. He held out his hand for Lydecker's glasses, his attention turned to the approaching column.

Clifton Ellis had his look, then

began to swear, softly, and with an old soldier's mastery of profanity. The column was near enough now to be identified without the glasses, and Ellis could only stare. Above the sounds of march music came the rumble of heavy wheels, gun carriages, limbers, wagons, each pulled by six massive horses.

"Artillery!" Clifton Ellis's voice was a bull-bellow. "I ask headquarters for a replacement of infantry and they send me a battery of damned horse artillery!" He seized the glasses again and restudied the approaching column, focusing his magnified vision on the man at the head. He seemed impatient to pin down the responsibility for this outrage.

And recognition came. "Mr. Lydecker," he said, "send a runner for Major Davis and have him report to my office immediately."

The OD turned to a trooper. "You, there! You heard that! On the double!" The trooper scampered down the ladder, running for the infirmary where Major Davis usually spent his time sampling the contract surgeon's stock of medicinal alcohol.

Colonel Ellis turned. "Send the new post commander to my office as soon as he's free."

"Yes, sir."

The colonel was already stomping down the ladder. He puffed across the parade, and when he mounted the steps he had to stop and brace himself while his strength returned. Then he went into the office and sat down.

Major Davis appeared. He was a small man, well put together. The brandy put a slight glaze to his eyes.

"Major, if you're sober enough to understand, the troops who are to activate Fort Runyon are arriving." He slapped his desk. "Artillery."

"Artillery, sir?" Davis laughed. "You're joking."

"I'm not joking," Ellis said. "And do you know who is in command?"

"No, sir. How would I know, sir?"

"Captain McCracken. I imagine you

remember Captain McCracken."

Major Davis's expression seemed to freeze. "Yes, sir. As the colonel knows, I have good cause to remember him."

Ellis drummed his fingers on his desk. "Major, I don't believe it would be for the good of the service if you and McCracken met head-on to resume your hostilities. I suppose you still believe you were unjustly accused."

"Yes, sir, I do."

"Major, you were drunk on duty."

"I had been drinking, sir. I wasn't drunk. A man is drunk when he can't walk."

"And not drunk when he staggers?" Ellis waved his hand. "I don't mean to debate the question with you, Davis. My only concern is to keep you and McCracken from quarreling over something that happened years ago." He puffed his cheeks. "Well, I'm not going to worry about it; that is the new commanding officer's problem, not mine. Personally, I'm going to clean out my desk and take the first available transportation back to civilization. See that the artillery is billeted on the parade tonight."

"Yes, sir."

"And Davis, don't stir up trouble because you have a grudge against McCracken."

"Sir!"

"Don't sir me. Get out now and sober up!"

Davis's salute was clipped, betraying his anger. He walked to the ramp, mounted, and stared out at the approaching column. They marched in flank, two precise rows. McCracken was in the lead as they approached the gate. Lydecker ordered it opened.

As the battery filed through, McCracken ordered them about, wheeling them like a crack drill team, and when they halted they were in perfect park order. Mike Janis was pulling his wagons free and the field-grade officers' wives dismounted with obvious relief. They stood in a group until their husbands

82

appeared, then walked toward officers' row, the skirts lifted slightly to clear the dust.

McCracken spoke to Sergeant Karopsik. "Give the battery 'at ease'." Then he spoke to the drummer. "'Officers' call,' please,"

The drum flammed. Borgnine, Chaffee, and O'Fallon hurried from their sections. McCracken said, "A cold welcome will be waiting for me; I know Brubaker and he'll assume immediate command. Stay here until I come back, and see that none of our men mix in with the cavalry or infantry on the post."

He supposed that he should have omitted the remark about Brubaker and himself, since it was not a military matter, yet he saw no reason to try to hide what was common knowledge.

The sutler's van drove on to headquarters and Colonel Truman Brubaker dismounted. He went inside as soon as the social amenities were exchanged with Colonel Ellis, who was damned glad to be leaving and made no bones about it.

McCracken decided that Brubaker's first official act would be to summon him to headquarters, and he was not mistaken. Lieutenant Lydecker hurried up. "The colonel's compliments, sir. He's waiting in his office."

McCracken excused himself and crossed through the parked battery to headquarters. An orderly was waiting and ushered him into Brubaker's new office.

"At ease, Robert," Brubaker said. "I won't lie and say that I enjoyed the trip." He leaned back and stared at McCracken. "I take my duty seriously; I don't think I need remind you of that."

"I'm aware of the colonel's feelings," McCracken said, "and because of this I would like to assume command of Fort Runyon and reactivate it against the Sioux threat."

"You're welcome to it," Brubaker told him. "You said exactly what I wanted you to say. You can leave in the morning."

"That soon, sir? The men have had a hard march and could use a few day's rest."

Brubaker smiled thinly. "Captain, am I to assume that this is an admission on your part that the artillery is a delicate arm?"

"No, sir," McCracken said flatly. "We'll depart in the morning."

"Fine," Brubaker said. "That's the kind of co-operation I expect." His smile was without humor. "It's been a long time since the war, Robert."

"Yes, sir. The colonel has a very long memory, sir," McCracken said.

"That is correct," Brubaker said. "And, Captain, I am not at all pleased with your artillery and my report will state that." He waved his hands. "General Staff will be waiting for approval or disapproval of your unit. I can tell you now what it will be, but I believe you know. No, Captain, I'm not going to sink you, but

I'm going to give you every chance to sink yourself. Only cavalry and infantry can reactivate and hold Fort Runyon, but you'll get a chance with your artillery. I'll send Glendennon along with a troop of cavalry, but you can defend the damned place any way you can with your machines."

McCracken felt strangely like a gift, boxed and wrapped. The colonel had left a door open for escape, which was McCracken's resignation. Resign and let Brubaker win, or stay and fight an impossible fight; and in the end Brubaker would win that too. Still, he felt a hard core of determination rise. "Thank you for the opportunity, sir," McCracken said.

"What's this?"

"I thanked you for the assignment, sir. Specifically, Fort Runyon."

Brubaker's eyes narrowed. "Once you made a fool of me in front of my superiors. That will never happen again, Captain. And you won't last long enough to prove the absurd claims you've made for artillery. Oh, I read them. You're making yourself the laughing stock of the army, but I'm not going to be a part of it. I could have transferred you before this, but I have plans for you, Robert." He paused to light a cigar. "Be a good soldier, but remember that you will never be good enough to suit me."

"I think I understand," McCracken said.

"Do you?" Brubaker smiled. "Captain, once you placed me in a most delicate position, where my orders and motives, yes, even my courage was examined minutely by the commanding generals. No officer likes that, Robert. I disliked it particularly. That's where I'm going to put you, where you will have to explain away the unexplainable. I'm going to officially question every move you make, every order you give, and when I'm through, I don't think the army will ever completely trust you again even with a wood-cutting detail."

"I see," McCracken said. His hands began to shake and he jammed them into his pockets. "Then why don't you get me and leave the artillery alone? Why drag it to obscurity just to get me?"

"A man has to be practical," Brubaker said. "Washington views your tactics with suspicion already. I can't ignore such an obvious crack in the door, can I?"

"You hate me that much, sir?"

"Let us just say that I distrust a man who does not make a mistake. You're excused, Captain."

McCracken saluted and went outside. The OD was talking to Borgnine when McCracken came up. McCracken gave his orders briefly and was then assigned quarters. The dismissal of an infantry company was simply a matter of telling the men to fall out and clean their rifles, but an artilleryman faced a different problem. There were animals to stable and groom, gun batteries to unlimber and trail, and wagons to park in the farrier sergeant's yard.

Because of this ponderous equipment, it was mid-afternoon before the 7th Light Artillery was secured to quarters. And by this time the word about Robert Duward McCracken's march through Chief Gall's forces had passed around the post.

After checking the barracks and stables, McCracken walked across the post to his own quarters and entered. Lieutenant Borgnine was squatting in a large wooden tub. He looked around as McCracken entered, then went on with his scrubbing. He said, "The dirt's an inch thick."

"Dirt comes off," McCracken said. He unbuckled his pistol belt and hung it on a wall peg. Then he stripped off his shirt, dropped his long underwear around his waist, and washed at the night stand. While he was drying, Lieutenant O'Fallon came in, threw his kepi on one of the bunks and sat down.

"That Fields Dandridge is talking up

a storm in the cavalry mess," O'Fallon said.

McCracken looked at him. "About me?"

"About nothing else, sir." O'Fallon smiled. "You made quite an impression on him, turning Gall back the way you did."

"What kind of an impression did I make on you?" McCracken asked. He saw O'Fallon flounder and realized that his question was unfair. "Forget it," he said. "Mr. Borgnine, we'll leave the post at seven in the morning. I'll contact Lieutenant Glendennon, who is in command of the cavalry. He's to go with us."

"And I thought we were going to get a rest," O'Fallon said.

"When did my command ever rest?" McCracken asked.

Borgnine got out of the tub and stood on the bare floor, a growing pool of water fanning away from his feet. He dried with an old army blanket, then slipped into his underwear. "What you need, O'Fallon, is a rich aunt with a summer house on Long Island and a yacht on Lake Skaneateles. You don't have the bones for military service."

"I'd as soon be doing my duty back East," he admitted.

The sudden opening of the door announced Lieutenant Wilson Chaffee, who did everything with a rush of energy. Chaffee slammed down on his bunk and cocked his feet on the cross member. McCracken said, "I haven't thanked you yet, Wilson, for the job you did. That was fine shooting."

"Thank you, sir. Sorry about that one burst, but they ran into it."

"Hardly your fault," McCracken said. He stropped his razor and lathered his face. He bladed one cheek clean with a deft stroke. McCracken's face was bony, the dark skin tight-drawn over the framework. He was a man with dignity; his manner reflected it, and men could read it in his eyes. "Gentlemen," he said, "reactivating a post is never pleasant, especially a place like Fort Runyon that was given up five years ago under pressure. Chief Gall made war until headquarters ordered Runyon evacuated, but now headquarters have decided that they made a mistake. Gall will fight for his rights, and I can't blame him, but as the new commanding officer I'm determined to whip him."

"What kind of co-operation will Colonel Brubaker give you?" Borgnine asked.

McCracken looked at him, then picked up a towel and wiped his face. "Don't expect anything from Brubaker. When we leave this post in the morning, we'll be on our own. If we hold Fort Runyon, we'll do it with light artillery and one troop of reluctant cavalry."

"That'll be doing something never done before," O'Fallon said. "Artillery is a siege weapon, sir. You'll have a hard time convincing Washington otherwise."

Gustave Borgnine stomped into his boots, then bent to grease them. "You just stick with the captain, O'Fallon. You'll learn a lot you never knew before."

Getting out his dispatch case, McCracken sat down to compose his report. Borgnine went out, and a few minutes later Wilson Chaffee left. O'Fallon was a man who liked his rest and soon was snoring a counterpoint to McCracken's scratching pen. For an hour he wrote without pause, then reread his report and folded it. Too bad, he thought, that it would never reach Washington.

He stepped outside, report in hand, and paused on the porch. Troopers were gathered around the parade perimeter, staring in silence at the artillery. He understood their feelings. Among soldiers there seemed a great dignity in meeting the enemy in close combat. Artillery never did this. To a soldier, artillery fought in a cowardly fashion, crouched below the protecting brow of a hill, flinging haphazard death at an unseen enemy. And this silent shame extended even to their own artillery, as though a member of the team had committed an unutterable foul.

Colonel Brubaker was not in his office, and the orderly directed McCracken to the colonel's quarters across the parade. Having no wish for further conversation with Brubaker, McCracken left the report with the orderly and walked to the officers' mess. Dandridge was still there, and McCracken took a seat across from him.

"Going along in the morning?" McCracken asked him.

"I wouldn't miss it," Dandridge said. He pushed his plate aside. "Captain, when I took this assignment, I'll admit it was to record your failure. But I want you to know that I'll take the greatest pride in reporting your success. Call it the last laugh if you want, but there's something about you that I think spells a winner."

"That's nice of you to say," McCracken said. "I hope it turns out your way, Mr. Dandridge."

"Is there any doubt, sir?"

McCracken smiled. "yes, it would appear a great deal." He considered telling Dandridge that the success of a command did not depend only on weapons or strength, although these were important, but the young man had been an able officer himself; he didn't need to be told. The success was always the commander's responsibility.

McCracken shifted a few of the dishes, placed the salt and pepper shakers in strategic spots, then said, "Fort Runyon is here, at the beginning of the plains. The mountains end here to the south; there's a natural pass there. The purpose in building the fort in the first place was to block this pass. Cavalry failed to do it. Infantry failed."

"But you think you can do it with artillery?"

McCracken frowned slightly. "Only partly, Mr. Dandridge. The post is really too far from the pass for complete defense. And too small. But I think I have an idea on how to correct that."

"How?"

"I'd rather not talk about it now, Mr. Dandridge."

"Sorry, sir."

"Forget it," McCracken said. "I can promise you a front row seat."

After mess, McCracken returned to his quarters and stretched out on the bunk for a rest. He listened to the changing sounds of the post. The army always took on a different tempo at night. He heard a detail moving by; that would be the second guard relief changing. From across the parade drifted the bee-hum of men talking in the mess. This was the sound of men relaxing, of men forgetting the thirty-five cents a day routine and of the years to go on their hitch, and the reupping because there was no place for them outside the 'system'. O'Fallon snored peacefully, sound asleep.

The night coolness filtered through the open door carrying a faint ammonia odor from the troop stables. When the shadows deepened, he got up and lighted the two wall lamps, then settled back again. Footfalls along the duckboards drew near, and he turned his head as Mike Janis came in.

"I'll leave if you're gettin' some shut-eye," Janis said. When McCracken shook his head, Janis sat down. He wore a pair of much patched pants, a shirt frayed at elbow and sleeve, and a battered hat. "You know I'm goin' along in the mornin', Bob?"

"No, I didn't," McCracken said.

"Three wagons with supplies," Janis said. "I'm goin' to take Marta along, Bob. I heard that Glendennon was taking his wife; Brubaker suggested it to him."

A furrow formed on McCracken's forehead. "Runyon was never a post for women," he said. "Especially now."

"I can't leave Marta," Mike said. "Too many sojers'll take a look at her, see that Crow blood, and figure they got a right to free use . . . " He paused a moment, sorting out the words. "Then there's this Dandridge fella. He keeps after her. I hear tell he's got enough money to buy the army. She needs a man like that, one that can lift her so high no one'll dare mention that she's half Injun."

"Maybe Dandridge isn't serious," McCracken said softly.

"He better be," Janis said. "Bob, she's all I got to my name and it's got to come out right for her." He paused, rubbing his hands together. "Wish you'd talk to her, Bob. She always listened to you, even when she was a little girl."

"That was years ago," McCracken pointed out. "Mike, she's a grown woman now, with a mind of her own."

"Talk to her anyway. As a favor to me, Bob."

"Sure," McCracken said.

Janis seemed relieved. He slapped his thighs and stood up. "Guess I'm keepin' you from your sleep." He went out immediately and McCracken listened to the dying thump of his boots along the duckboards.

He turned his thoughts to Colonel Truman Brubaker and his insane suggestion that Glendennon take his wife along. McCracken was not a suspicious man, but this was so out of place . . .

He waited a few minutes, then put on his kepi and walked slowly to the rear of the sutler's store. Through the window he saw Marta at the stove. He knocked and she opened the door for him.

"This is unexpected," she said.

"I hope I'm not intruding," McCracken said.

"You're always welcome, Bob." She took his hat and offered him a chair at the table. "Care for some coffee and cake?"

"Fine." He watched her move about, as lithe as a fawn, and beneath her slenderness was a finely honed strength. She put the plate and cup before him, then took a chair opposite so she could face him.

Suddenly she said, "I feel easy with you, Bob. Is that because I've known you for so long?"

"Perhaps it's because you can think of me as an old man of thirty-one."

She laughed easily. "That's not it at all. I guess I don't have to hide anything from you, Bob."

"What's there to hide, Marta?"

"I'm half Indian," she said. "That makes me different."

"For a mixed-up young woman," he said, "you make good cake."

When he finished his coffee, he stood up and took his hat from the wall peg. Marta said, "Do you have to go?"

"Early start in the morning." He smiled. "Stop thinking so much, Marta."

He went out, closing the door softly, then cut across the parade. Ahead, he saw a man standing, the red tip of his cigar glowing and dying. When McCracken approached, Harry Glendennon took the cigar from his lips and said, "Captain McCracken?"

"Yes?"

100

"I'd like a moment of your time," He offered a cigar, but the captain shook his head. "I was a little short with you about my wife. Actually I'm very much indebted to you, Captain."

"Not at all," McCracken said. "Likely we'll see a lot of each other at Fort Runyon. I'm looking forward to a pleasant association."

"With me or my wife?"

"Why, you clumsy ass!" McCracken said before check-reining his temper. When he spoke again, his voice was evenly controlled. "Lieutenant, if you have any personal difficulties with your wife, I suggest that you keep them within the confines of your quarters. Don't try to involve me, Mr. Glendennon. You can take that as a flat warning."

With a curt nod, McCracken moved past Glendennon and went on to his own quarters. Glendennon's remark irritated McCracken out of all proportion to its importance. That the man had the nerve to assume that there was anything romantic . . . He shook his head as if to straighten out his thoughts, and entered his quarters.

Chaffee and O'Fallon were in the bunks asleep, and as McCracken undressed, Lieutenant Borgnine came in. McCracken did not speak, and since Borgnine's acquaintance was of long standing, he sensed his commanding officer's mood and respected the silence.

McCracken settled down and Borgnine snuffed out the lamps. Straw ticks rustled a bit, then silence moved into the room, broken only by the regular breathing of O'Fallon, who had the unfortunate habit of sleeping with his mouth open.

★ ★ ★

Reveille woke them, but McCracken was already up and about, his breakfast eaten and orders given to Sergeant Karopsik. In an hour and a half McCracken's company was ready for the march, waiting on the parade ground while Lieutenant Glendennon gathered his troops of cavalry.

Mike Janis's three wagons were tucked in between double rows of artillery caissons, and as Glendennon prepared to mount his troop, Colonel Brubaker stomped importantly across the parade. He offered his hand to Glendennon and deliberately ignored McCracken. This was in full view of the complement of the post and the captain felt blood vault into his face.

"I'll expect dispatches," Brubaker said, moving near McCracken. His glance touched the poised and glistening machines. "I give you no longer than three weeks, Captain, before Chief Gall runs you out of there."

"Suppose we wait and see, Colonel. Meanwhile, I can expect negative reports on my record?"

"You may certainly rely on that," Brubaker said. "Don't think I'm unaware of the Department's thinking. The campaign is expected to go badly and by sending you with these hopeless

103

pieces of junk, they mean to make a scapegoat of me in the event of failure."

A shrewdness came into McCracken's eyes. He realized that this was as pat an excuse as an officer could ask for, especially if he meant to whitewash himself while he painted someone else black. He bent forward and spoke so only Brubaker could hear. "Colonel, for years you've had a knife sharpened for my scalp. Suppose you just swing at me and leave the artillery alone."

"Why should I do that?"

"It would be easier for you to get me than the whole corps. Besides, a man of your rank is not without influence." He saw amusement in Brubaker's eyes, but he went on anyway. "You've never been a man to act without cause, Colonel. What, besides satisfaction, do you gain by ruining me?"

"To me that is enough."

"But suppose I save Fort Runyon for you, and in that way save this campaign?"

"Impossible."

"But suppose," McCracken insisted. "Can I count on a reversal of your opinion, Colonel?"

"I never make a bargain with a man who is certain to fail, Captain. And as sure as you sit there, you are going to fail. That's a promise I've made myself, and you know I always keep a promise."

"Yes, I think that's pretty well settled," McCracken said, and turned his attention to the movement of his command. At his signal the detail stirred like a waking dog, ripples of movement flowing from one end to the other. The gates were open and they passed from the post onto the vast land. Glendennon's cavalry paraded to the flanks with a great air of superiority while McCracken's battery lumbered forth, filling the air with dust and sound. A portion of the cavalry troop formed the point a mile in advance of the main column while the rest deployed on the flanks.

Colonel Brubaker mounted the palisade ramp and studied the command as it moved away from the post. His bland eyes were expressionless as he regarded the dwindling column. Ten years before, during the Rebellion, he had observed many columns, but mostly infantry and cavalry. Artillery had used the back roads and had traveled at night as though there were some shame attached to them that could not bear the light of day. Brubaker had been cavalry then, as had McCracken, and to Brubaker's way of thinking a man should remain loyal to his first branch of the service, which, in a way, made McCracken a traitor.

With unnerving clarity Brubaker could recall that day near Miller's Falls; the order to retreat had been clearly given, yet McCracken had taken the hill, leaving Brubaker to make stupidly lame excuses to three generals. Generals whom he had convinced, not three hours before, that taking the Confederate position was impossible.

That day, in Brubaker's opinion, was the turning point in his military career. The generals had told him that he was blameless; at least it said so on his record, but he knew differently. They remembered the incident every time a good command turned up, and gave it to someone else. He knew that he had been given this command only because the situation was considered hopeless.

A proving ground for harebrained theories; he hated the thought, and also the man sent here to prove them. Within Brubaker's mind burned a longing to restore himself to the position he had enjoyed before he met McCracken. This was cavalry country, and only cavalry campaigns would succeed here. If he could prove that to Washington, he could vindicate himself, restore himself, and if he had to destroy another man and his dreams to do it, then he would and consider the price cheap.

With this comforting thought in mind,

Colonel Truman Brubaker stepped down from the palisade wall and walked across the parade to his office.

★ ★ ★

The distance to Fort Runyon was sixty-four miles as McCracken remembered it. Two days, if he pushed, and he intended to do just that. By mid-morning a river was crossed and only through careful attention to detail did McCracken's officers keep the gun carriages from bogging down. On the north shore, Glendennon set a pace carefully calculated to wear the artillery down, but after fifteen miles it was the cavalry that had to dismount and lead. The heavy draught horses had the staying power the smaller cavalry mounts lacked.

In the early afternoon McCracken saw the first sign of Indians, a spiraling smoke column on the buttes to the west. Chaffee, who was always alert, saw it at the same moment and signaled Glendennon, who had missed it completely.

Riding back to Mike Janis's wagon, McCracken enlisted his services as a scout, putting the old man on the point with the cavalry. During the rest of the day they drove north and that evening camped where McCracken thought an attack was least likely to occur, backed against the south fork of the Wind River.

There was the business of squad fires and pickets; it was fully dark before he was ready to eat. Mike Janis and Marta sat before McCracken's fire, and as the captain washed his hands, Fields Dandridge came up and dismounted.

"Enough for a fourth?" he asked. "Glendennon's poor company; he's arguing with his wife."

"Fetch a tin plate," McCracken said. He did not want to discuss Glendennon's domestic difficulty, nor have Dandridge discuss it.

The meal was beef stew, biscuits and coffee, and a healthy appetite made it tasty. Dandridge had two helpings, then leaned back with his coffee. "What do you make of the smoke, Captain? Gall?"

"Yes," McCracken said. "I don't expect trouble, though. He'll let us through to Fort Runyon. Be easier to attack us when we're bottled up at the fort."

"A pretty grim thought," Dandridge said softly. "But Gall can't whip the whole army. Doesn't he know that?"

"Sure," McCracken said, "but this isn't the whole army, and even if it were he'd try. You can see that." He leaned back, an arm hooked around his raised knee.

"This used to be Crow country, then the Sioux began to push them out. A lot of wars were fought here before the white men came. And when they saw the country, they began to shove the Sioux out, which hasn't been too easy."

"Not much justice to it, is there?" Dandridge asked.

"That's not really for you and me to decide," McCracken said. "I take whatever orders come my way. When the day comes that I can't take them, I'll resign my commission." He stood up then, indicating his desire to turn in. Mike and Marta went to their own camp, but Fields Dandridge remained.

"Captain, you've known Marta Janis a long time, haven't you?"

"Since she was five," McCracken said. "Mike brought her to civilization then."

"I like her, Captain, but she can't see me. Is there a reason?"

"You'll have to ask her," McCracken said gently. He touched Dandridge on the arm. "You're moving too fast for her. Give it time."

"All right," Dandridge said, and went to his own camp.

The day's march had worn the conversation out of every man, and quiet descended quickly, broken only by the movements of the horse herd and guards walking their posts. Fires died, one by one, and the camp slept. Meanwhile, on the high ground, hostile eyes kept watch through the night.

McCracken had his command breakfasted and on the move by sunup. Through a hot day they marched north, following the old trail, and in the late afternoon they raised the half-crumbled walls of Fort Runyon.

Edging down out of the pass, McCracken studied the fort, nearly a mile away. Beyond, the land spread to the horizon, unbroken by hills or timber. All during the day he had been watching for signs of Chief Gall and his warriors, but they seemed to have disappeared.

Suddenly, from around a jutting rock promontory, a stream of mounted Sioux rode into the clear. Everyone saw them and the cavalry wheeled, looking to McCracken for orders, but he indicated by a wave of his hand that the march was to continue. Gall had his men in a long column, perhaps a mile and a half ahead, but his intention was clear enough. He intended to deny the column access to the fort.

From the point, Glendennon and Mike Janis wheeled back, drawing up on McCracken's right. Glendennon said, "Dammit, Captain, I can't ride through a force like that."

"I didn't ask you to," McCracken said. He turned in the saddle. "Mr. Borgnine, come here, please." When the heavy-set officer pulled up, McCracken said, "Drop your section out and take a position along the trail. We'll use our advancing maneuver."

"Yes, sir."

Glendennon spoke his disgust. "Advancing maneuver! We'll never advance through them!"

This was the type of argument McCracken hated. He pitched his voice to the tone of a general's. "Mr. Glendennon, if you can restrain yourself a moment, I'll give you some orders. Proceed in a column of twos as though you meant to engage Gall. Draw him out if you can but under no circumstances are you to close any more than two hundred and fifty yards. Is that understood? Two hundred and fifty yards. If you disobey that order, I won't be able to save you."

"Save me? Why, you stuffed, over-bloated, egotistical — "

He got no further. McCracken whipped his hand across Glendennon's face. The sutler's wagons were going by and from the corner of his eye, McCracken saw Sheila Glendennon's shocked expression, but this did not distract him. "Mr. Glendennon," he said, "that was a direct order. Carry it out or, by God, I'll have you shot."

Trembling, Glendennon wheeled his horse and rode furiously toward his waiting command. McCracken then summoned Lieutenant Chaffee forward, and when the young officer sided him, said, "You know what to do, Mr. Chaffee. Bore straight through behind the cavalry and when Gall's men break for Mr. Borgnine, fall out and unlimber."

"Fire in front of them, sir?"

"For the record this time," McCracken said. "Gall wants a fight, well, we'll give him one."

His command was rushing past, gathering momentum as it tore off the last remaining slope, and McCracken gigged his horse into motion and raced with it. Far ahead now, the cavalry under Glendennon was charging at Gall's arrayed warriors, while behind the column Gustave Borgnine stood alone on the slope with his section, two guns being unlimbered and set up for action.

Glendennon and his troops were closing at a fast rate, then suddenly Borgnine opened up with his cannon. Over the din of rumbling wheels and thundering hoofs, McCracken heard the peculiar *whoosh* of banded shells tearing through the air, then spouts of earth rose amid the thunder claps, and the Sioux broke their line and began to mill while warriors fought to check their terrified horses. But the fear was not limited to the Sioux. Harry Glendennon's cavalry charge broke like a dry twig and nearly scatterd; the thought of friendly artillery whirring over his head was too sudden and terrifying to ignore.

McCracken cursed the man in a loud voice but did not slacken his advance speed. Borgnine's section was firing again, sending shells into the Sioux front ranks which had split and were flanking at a distance. Suddenly McCracken and his command were into the cavalry, sweeping it along and through the new gap in the enemy line. They ran on for perhaps a quarter of a mile, then Chaffee suddenly wheeled out of the column with his section, plowed to a halt and dropped trails.

Signaling, McCracken gathered his forces and brought them about and to a halt. Borgnine was still on the hill, limbering for a fast run toward McCracken, but blocking him was a charging wave of hostile Sioux. Deprived of a victory over the main force, they were now intent on wiping out Borgnine's lone section.

Chaffee hardly needed a command to fire. Lanyards were yanked and iron-shod wheels bucked off the ground. The guns were fired in relays with only seconds between shots. Ahead of the racing Sioux, a geyser of dirt spouted high, then another as Chaffee got the range. He was laying his barrage exactly in between Borgnine and the enemy, and in this way sealed Borgnine off from them. He dropped his elevation slightly and sent the next two rounds into the Indians' midst, breaking them effectively. The noise of their frustrated shouting was a din that overrode the boom of the artillery; then they charged off to the east, leaving a clear field for Borgnine who raced toward McCracken's position. Chaffee kept up his fire, laying a line of explosives to keep the Sioux from charging Borgnine.

But Borgnine was too far out of their range now. McCracken shouted,

"Cease firing! Swab bores, Mr. Chaffee. And congratulations on the shooting."

Fields Dandridge came up from the right flank, and from the cavalry section Harry Glendennon rode forward at a gallop. McCracken turned toward him as Dandridge shouted, then Glendennon left his saddle, dove across McCracken's horse, and carried the tall captain to the ground.

The fall nearly jarred McCracken senseless, but anger gave him strength to get to his feet as Glendennon rolled free and charged, arms windmilling. There was only fury to the man, no control. McCracken ducked and struck Glendennon solidly in the mouth with his fist.

The blow shocked him to a standstill. McCracken drove his fist into the man's stomach, and when he bent over, McCracken straightened him with an uppercut that started low and ended suddenly. Glendennon's back whipped into a bow and he tottered, falling with arms outspread.

McCracken looked at him for a moment; every man watched. Then he poured water from his canteen into Glendennon's face and watched him stir. The lieutenant looked at McCracken, hate flooding his eyes as he lay there.

"You wanted . . . to kill . . . me," he said hoarsely. "You want her that bad?"

"You're out of your mind," McCracken said.

"Shooting over us . . . you could have hit us." He raised a hand to paw at the blood seeping from his nose. "You wanted to kill me so you could have her for yourself."

The wagons were drawn up near by, and Sheila Glendennon observed all this in white-faced silence. McCracken knew she could hear but this did not stop him. "Get to your feet," he snapped. Glendennon obeyed, but with purposeful sluggishness. "Stand at attention."

There was a whip in McCracken's

voice, the inherent ability to command that he always doubted he had, and this snapped Glendennon stiff. "Mr. Glendennon, you are a miserable coward." He watched the young officer's face blanch, knew that he was permanently damaging the man, but he didn't know of any other way to handle this. "The only reason I'm not going to have you court-martialed is that I'm in desperate need of officers, even a specimen like you. Anything to say?"

"I'm sorry," Glendennon mumbled. "I guess I lost my head."

"That is not an officer's privilege," McCracken said.

"It was those shells, sir. They passed so close overhead. I'd have sworn that you were shooting at me."

"Your fear is understandable," McCracken said, "but not your conduct."

"Yes, sir." Glendennon stood at attention and realized that his anger, although spontaneous, was also working for the colonel's private purpose; he wished that he could separate the two and reserve his own anger for his own benefit.

"Mr. Glendennon, please bear in mind that you've not only disgraced yourself, but brought shame to every man in your troop. You are going to have to prove and re-prove yourself to those men before they'll ever trust you again." He waved his hand. "You're excused, Mr. Glendennon." This last remark, McCracken decided was something he could have left unsaid, yet he felt a driving need to break the man, and at the same time was ashamed that he could feel this way about anybody.

Glendennon stumbled slightly as he moved away. When he passed the wagon in which his wife was seated he stopped and looked at her but she quickly turned away and went beneath the canvas cover. McCracken watched him, regret in his expression. Fields Dandridge stood in silence as did Borgnine, Chaffee and O'Fallon.

Borgnine was the one to speak. "I never saw you do that before, sir, chew a man in front of his men. I'm not saying he didn't have it coming, but — "

"Let's forget it," McCracken said quickly. He looked back along the trail they had just traveled. High on the hill sat Gall and his warriors.

Chaffee said, "Like sitting ducks, sir. We could sweep that hill clean at a mile."

"We'll keep the range of our weapons a secret a little longer," McCracken said. "Mr. Borgnine, move the column on to Fort Runyon."

"Yes, sir."

They all moved away, except Fields Dandridge. McCracken turned to him. "Did you get something to write about, Mr. Dandridge?"

"Sure did," Dandridge said. "But one of the stories I'll never write."

"Thank you. But it's within your rights to do so, if you wish."

"I don't wish," Dandridge said. "Glendennon's got enough to live with. Besides, I didn't come out here to make things tough for anyone."

McCracken's smile was quick and genuine. "I think I like you, Fields." He clapped the young man on the shoulder, then went into the saddle, moving out at a trot to catch up with the head of the column.

Fort Runyon, even in its brief span of existence, had never been much. Troopers detested it for its cramped accommodations, and officers disliked it for its impossible position, too far away from the pass it was meant to defend.

The gate hung on rotting leather hinges, and the weather had ruined nearly all of one adobe wall. McCracken gathered his command on the weed-choked parade and dismounted them.

"Lieutenant Chaffee," he said, "make a survey of the post and report to me."

While Chaffee was about this business,

McCracken disbursed his command and parked his artillery. Within a half-hour, Chaffee came back.

"The south, west, and north walls are sound, sir."

"How are the buildings?"

"They all need repair. Mostly roofs and windows."

"The stables secure?"

"Fairly sound," Chaffee said. "Shall I assemble a work detail?"

"Yes. Let Glendennon and the cavalry take care of the stables and farrier's yard. Get two sections on the wall in the morning. I want a full guard tonight. A man every eight feet."

"Yes, sir."

"What about quarters for the women?"

"They can be made to do," Chaffee said.

"Carry on then," McCracken said, and went about the hundred details confronting him. There were the supply wagons to unload, and a field kitchen to set up until the mess was put in running condition.

Darkness came on almost unnoticed and it was almost eight before he could sit down to his supper and relax. The post was not large enough to park his artillery within the parade confines. All of the buildings except headquarters huddled against the mud walls, and the roof of each became the walkway on which the guards paced back and forth. Not an arrangement to promote sleep, he decided, and made a mental note to change that. Timber was available just four miles away, and with a troop of cavalry to cover a wood-cutting detail he could rebuild most of the fort in a more substantial fashion.

By ten o'clock the post had settled into silence for the night, and Captain McCracken left his quarters for a final tour. The guards were pacing their stations along the remaining palisade walls, and as McCracken moved about he noticed a shadow move near the main gate. Without apparent haste he walked in that direction, then stopped when he recognized Sheila Glendennon.

"I couldn't sleep," she said. "Tramping feet on the roof kept me awake."

"I'll walk you back to your quarters," he said, taking her arm.

She shrugged and turned with him. "That was a nice tactical move this afternoon."

For an instant he didn't know what to say. "I'm sorry about your husband, but he left me little choice."

"Don't apologize," she said quickly. "He doesn't deserve it," He looked at her quickly, a bit shocked and she shook her head. "Don't look so surprised. I'm not in love with him and I'm going to divorce him."

Her offhand coldness offended McCracken. She sounded as though she were discussing the personal failings of some distant relative, not a man she had promised to love. "Have you told him this?"

"Not yet," she said. "I'll wait until he's sober."

"Sober? Is he drunk?"

"Of course he's drunk. When Harry makes a fool of himself, he becomes ashamed. And Harry can't face himself feeling ashamed, so he gets good and drunk. In the morning he'll be even more ashamed and tell me how no good he is and how I'm wasting my life on him and why I ought to just leave or divorce him. Of course, he doesn't mean all those things. It's just his way to gain my reassurance. Only this time I'm going to surprise him."

"Sounds pretty cold and calculated," McCracken said.

"It is. Just as cold and calculated as you were when you ripped into him this afternoon." They approached her quarters and stopped before her door. For a moment she was silent, then she said, "I think I'd like to be kissed, Robert."

This was a dare, he knew, as he listened to the small warning stirring in his mind. Her lips were soft and very inviting and he could not mistake her intent. Reluctantly he held his arms to his sides and stepped back.

"You made a mistake," he said. "Don't make it again."

"That's all in the point of view," she said softly. "Will you come in?"

"No, I guess not."

She seemed amused. "You're an honorable man, Robert, but you don't owe any of it to Harry." She canted her head to one side. "Have I shocked you? I didn't mean to. It's just that I believe a person should ask for what they want."

"I don't think you know what you want," McCracken said. "You're a married woman, Sheila. Maybe not in your mind, but by law you are."

"Yes," she said, "and it's too damned bad." With that she turned and went inside, closing the door.

McCracken returned slowly to his own quarters. He did not bother to light the lamp but stripped off his shirt in the darkness, hanging his gunbelt on the bedpost. The parade was a silent patch of parked guns as he went to the open door to stand for a moment, looking out.

From the darkness behind him Mike Janis spoke softly, making McCracken start. "Thought I'd scare you, so I waited until you hung up your pistol."

McCracken found a lantern and raised the glass dropping it back when Janis said, "The dark suits me, Bob, unless it bothers you."

"It doesn't bother me," McCracken said, and sat down on the bunk. "Something eating you, Mike?"

"Injuns," Janis said. "They always fret me, 'specially Sioux." He sighed heavily. "When I was young, I loved a Crow woman. Married her and was one of the tribe. But a man changes when he gets older. I give up the Injuns. Even the Crows." McCracken could hear him patting his pockets and handed him a cigar. There was a flare from a match, then darkness again except for the red end and the sudden aroma of Kentucky twist. "Gall took a lickin' from you this afternoon, Bob. Likely he'll be wantin' another chance before a new moon shines."

"I'll be here," McCracken said. "When he wants me, all he'll have to do is come and get me."

"And I guess he will," Janis said. "But what's it goin' to settle?"

"If I can only convince him of the hopelessness of fighting," McCracken said, "maybe a new treaty can be made."

"Too late for that," Janis said. "Too many treaties been made and broken for Gall to ever trust a white man's paper." He shook his head. "Kind of sad, Bob. I mean, the way it's got to turn out. Was you to tell Gall that you had him licked, he'd laugh at you, because he already knows that. He knew it when Wessell whipped Red Cloud. It's just that one of you has to end up dead before this thing is put down."

He went to the door and stopped as McCracken said, "Wait, Mike, what am

I going to do about communications?"

"Union Pacific's working near Laramie," Janis said. "A rider could get through. Gall can't watch you all the time, or in every direction."

"One man every week?"

Janis shrugged. "Can you spare a man a week?"

"What do you mean?"

"I mean it's a one-way trip," Janis said. "You wouldn't ask a man to ride back after he sneaked through the Injun country, would you?"

"No," McCracken said. "Can you work out a good route for a courier? A safe one. I can't afford to waste men, especially when I won't get them back."

"Yup." There was amusement in his voice. "Ol' Brunbaker ain't goin' to like this, Bob. I guess he's countin' on sendin' in his own reports on top of your own."

"Let him send them," McCracken said.

"Whoa now. You're stickin' your neck

131

way out. Brubaker's the commanding officer and if you go over his head and — "

"I don't intend to do that," McCracken said. "*My* reports will go to Brubaker and through channels." He grinned. "But I got an observer here, Mike. Fields Dandridge. He'll want to send dispatches of his own."

"By God, that's pretty slick," Janis said. He started out the door and paused again. "Seen you with the lieutenant's wife. Ain't you got enough trouble now?"

"More than enough and that's what I told her," McCracken said. "You worry too much, Mike."

"Someone has to." He went out then with his shuffling gait and McCracken lay back on his bunk. There was a seasoned wisdom in Janis and the advice he gave was offered only to his closest friends. Advice worth taking, but McCracken knew that the end decision would always be his to make, alone.

He turned his mind to the reconstruction of the post and the details served to absorb some of his ever present doubts. Finally sleep came in snatches, not a very restful sleep. When the drummer sounded reveille the next morning, he got up feeling as though he had just broken four cavalry mounts in succession.

The business of reactivating a dead post was an exacting one, with no margin for error. While details cut sod blocks for the walls, others rode into the timber and cut logs, dragging them back to the fort where they were sawed into planks or planted in the ground for buttresses to reinforce the wall.

During the week and a half following McCracken's arrival, his time was occupied from morning to late at night, and he had little time for anything except his job. With the fort in a fairly sound condition, he turned his attention to the construction of two large block-houses, nearly two hundred yards from the main gate and an equal distance apart.

The placing of these blockhouses was a fussy affair as far as McCracken was concerned, and his insistence that their position be surveyed exactly irritated Lieutenant O'Fallon, who was in charge of this work.

Lieutenant Glendennon had not spoken to McCracken since the trouble on the fort road, but he seemed to carry on his assignments with great care. Borgnine, who was second in command, relayed all orders to Glendennon, then checked frequently to see that they were carried out. Not once did he catch Glendennon in a mistake; the man had apparently stopped making them.

Then Captain McCracken ordered the digging begun, and the vast store of timbers he'd had cut found a purpose. From the center of the parade, a shaft was sunk for a distance of fifteen feet, a large shaft ten feet square. Then a tunnel was dug and carefully shored, a tunnel leading to each of the blockhouses. All dirt removed was taken by wagon, under cover of darkness, and dumped into the creek a mile below the fort. This went on for ten days, and McCracken's surveying paid off. At his direction, the tunnel roof was carved away and the men found that they exited in the blockhouses.

Along the hills bordering the pass, silent and careful observers studied each movement made inside the fort, and many times McCracken had caught the glint of sunlight on the field glass lens as Chief Gall made his study. But McCracken was sure that he had the Indians baffled, not only by the construction of the blockhouses, but by his conspicuous avoidance of them after they were built.

Gall didn't know that McCracken, with the help of an A-frame and a four-part purchase, had lowered two of his artillery pieces into the tunnel, run them by hand along its length, and rehoisted them inside the blockhouses.

Ammunition, water, rations, medical supplies; all these were stored in each of the blockhouses, making Fort Runyon actually three forts in one.

With reconstruction done, McCracken could now re-examine every move he had made for possible flaws. Flaws that Colonel Brubaker would love to magnify to threatening proportions. Living under the microscope of another man's dislike rankled McCracken, and many times he thought of the peace his resignation would bring. Yet he knew he could never resign. There was a difference between surrender and being licked.

* * *

Finally Chief Gall's curiosity got the better of him. Sporting a white flag, he made a ceremony of coming off the pass, a half dozen braves arrayed in finery behind him. McCracken saw this from the palisade wall. He turned and called to Borgnine, who was crossing the parade. "Park two wagons over the tunnel openings, and make damn sure that none of the planks show beneath the dirt covering."

"Right," Borgnine said, and called for Sergeant Karopsik.

Mike and Marta Janis came up the ladder to stand beside McCracken. "Are you going to let him in?" Marta asked.

"Why not?" McCracken said. "He's busting a gut to see what's going on. Indians like to talk, and one way to convince him that I have nothing to hide is to let him in. If I refuse, he'll be sure that I'm trying to trick him. I don't dare refuse him."

"One look around," Mike Janis said, "and he'll be able to give you a duty report better'n your first sergeant."

"He already knows our strength," McCracken said. "He just can't figure out what those blockhouses are for, Mike."

"You better hope he don't," Janis said, "or they'll get burned out."

There was no more talk as Chief Gall and his warriors approached at a slow walk. Gall was a magnificent specimen of a man, over six feet, barrel-chested, and with a face as haughty as a grand duke. He wore no headdress and was naked to the waist. His doeskin breeches were modestly beaded, but his Henry rifle was feathered near the muzzle and many brass tacks decorated the buttstock.

"Open the gates," McCracken said, then went down the ladder in time to meet Gall as he paused just inside the wall. His warriors remained outside; he was too smart a man to put all his protection on one side of the wall.

There was recognition in his eyes as he looked steadily at Robert McCracken and old hatreds flamed up. He would not make the sign for peace, and McCracken smiled; he could understand an enemy as unforgiving as Gall. This thought came as a surprise, because Truman Brubaker's hatred was as intense as Gall's. Yet the Indian's was infinitely more honest. There was no pretence in Gall, no clouded thinking. In the Indian's eyes, McCracken had inflicted a grievous hurt and Gall's honor demanded revenge; when he achieved it, the hatred would end. Brubaker, a more complex man would hate McCracken's memory if the young officer fell dead on the spot. McCracken supposed that was the price of civilization, and in that moment he pondered the value of it.

"Get down," he said. "Talk on your feet, Gall." There was purpose behind McCracken's demand; he wanted Gall to stand on the stiff leg, knowing that the Indian expected to have salt rubbed into his fester. McCracken was not going to disappoint him.

Slowly, indolently, Gall slid from his horse and stood with the grass rope rein in his hand. The Henry rifle was still cradled in his arm, the hammer back, and probably a live round waiting under it. "Years have passed, Red Hair, since these eyes have seen you."

"But you remember me when you walk," McCracken said. His eyes dropped to Gall's left leg; he was favoring it slightly by leaning a little to the right.

"Though my years be many," Gall said, "I will not forget." His dark eyes moved past McCracken to the parked artillery. "I have come to see these wagon guns."

"Look all you want," McCracken said. "If you wish to see how they work, line up your bucks about a half mile out and I'll show you."

"Big medicine," Gall said. "Before, wagon guns make big noise, do no harm. All time Carrington at Kearney, shoot wagon guns into woods, scare out Sioux. Not one Sioux die by wagon guns."

"How many died when you tried to attack me on the Fetterman road?"

Gall's face tightened. "Not many die. Maybe one. Maybe two." He looked at the assembled soldiers. "You lose many. Not many left — "

"You lie," McCracken said. "That one burst killed at least eight." He crossed his arms and rocked back on his heels. "You want peace, Gall? You want to bury the hatchet?"

"No peace now," Gall said. "Crazy Horse gone. Red Cloud gone. Sitting Bull go north. Only Chief Gall remains, Red Hair. I will fight you until one of us is dead."

McCracken glanced at Mike Janis, then at Gall. "Yo've been to the white man's school, even learned to read and write. You're a smart man. Do you think you can whip the whole army?"

"Gall not a fool," he said flatly. "Know cannot win big fight. But many little fights I will win. Maybe you be in little fight."

"This trail's going to open up," McCracken said. "Settlers are going to come through this land. We're here to see that they pass through without a lot of killing."

Gall tipped his head back and struck his chest, singing out a ringing whoop

141

over the still parade. "Many miles between pass and long knives' Fort Fetterman, Red Hair. Many miles to travel. Wagons not get through. Some, maybe, but many not get through." He made a sweep with his arm, indicating the vast plain beyond. "Many miles to white man's town, Red Hair. Wagons who get through to here, never reach town from here."

He had had his say and, in Indian fashion, he vaulted onto his pony and dashed from the post. The guards standing near the main gate lunged at him, but they slumped back when McCracken said, "Let him go!"

"Damn fool!" Mike Janis said. "You ought to've put a bullet in him and ended your trouble." He held up his hand. "I know, that white flag. A man's principles will kill him quicker'n anything." He turned away, a little disgusted.

Marta remained. "I hope you don't think Gall was bluffing, Bob."

McCracken put his hand on her

shoulder and smiled. "No, I don't think that. Come to headquarters with me." As they walked, McCracken spoke to a corporal in passing. "Find Mr. Chaffee and have him report to me in my office."

His office was a barren cubicle containing a minimum of furniture, all repaired by the battery carpenter. Marta sat down in the lone chair; McCracken perched on the corner of the desk, a leg dangling. "Are you still fighting with Fields Dandridge?" he asked.

Marta looked at him briefly. "I wouldn't fight with him, Bob." She pulled her eyes away. "He's making a mistake with me, that's all."

"What do you mean?" McCracken asked. "Marta, are you sure you don't have it twisted around?"

"Maybe I have," she admitted. "But I know what I'm doing. Fields is too nice to have regrets later." She stopped talking when Lieutenant Chaffee came across the porch.

"You wanted to see me, sir?"

"I have a job for you," McCracken said. "Strictly volunteer."

"Fine," Chaffee said. His youth gave him enthusiasm and he had the courage to carry it through.

McCracken opened his map case and tacked a large area map onto the rough planked wall. "Mr. Chaffee, it's my personal opinion that a thousand soldiers couldn't lick Chief Gall. Not only is he a superior fighter, but he has the advantage of lifetime familiarity with this terrain. An all out campaign against him, such as Colonel Brubaker would like to see me involved in, is doomed to failure. I believe he knows it, and that knowledge will soon be extended to departmental headquarters." He pointed to the pass leading from Fetterman to Fort Runyon. "This is the best wagon trail into Montana, and want to or not, it must be opened. Settlers are piling up at Platte Station and once they hear that there's a chance to get through, there'll be a steady stream through here."

"If Gall doesn't stop them," Chaffee said.

"I may be able to tend to that too," McCracken said. "Gall hates me personally because I once did him an injury and, in his eyes, I have never been punished for it. A strange thing about an Indian is his utter simplicity, Mr. Chaffee. Gall would pass up a chance to raid a settlers' wagon train if he thought it would give him a crack at me. And this is what I intend to do, give him a crack at me every time a wagon train leaves Fetterman."

Chaffee was genuinely puzzled. "But how will you know, sir?"

"You'll tell me," McCracken said flatly. "Mr. Chaffee, I want you to become a courier between Runyon and Fetterman. I'll make up a dispatch for you to carry to Brubaker, outlining the plan. He has a telegraph and he can invite wagon traffic. A troop of cavalry can accompany them to Fort Runyon. Naturally, you would come along with them most of the way, but then you would make a fast march here, inform me of the approximate arrival, and I'll try to decoy Gall. In the event he only splits his force, half to the wagons and half to me, I will at least have weakened him to the point where the wagons and cavalry may be able to take care of themselves." He paused a moment. "Once here, Glendennon's troop will take the wagons on, leaving the Fetterman cavalry here in it's place. Of course, Brubaker will not be able to let another convoy of wagons through until you return to Fort Fetterman."

McCracken hoped that his voice carried the necessary conviction, because he did not care to tell Chaffee why he thought the plan would work. Yet he knew that it would, with Brubaker's malicious blessing. Since McCracken intended to assume full responsibility for it, Brubaker would co-operate fully, hoping — and believing — that McCracken had at last bitten off too much to swallow. And that was possible, too, McCracken had to admit.

"I'm going to be doing a lot of riding," Chaffee said.

"A lot of dangerous riding. Report here after evening mess. I'll have dispatches for you and one of Glendennon's best horses."

Marta left with Chaffee and he began to write a lengthy report, slanted at Truman Brubaker's ego. An hour passed and dragged into two, then he raised his head as boots banged the loose porch planks and Fields Dandridge stepped inside.

"Captain, I'd like to talk to you."

McCracken laid his pen aside. "Then talk."

Dandridge sat down and laced his fingers together. "I heard that Lieutenant Chaffee is going to be a dispatch rider. And that's something I wanted to talk about." He paused and McCracken waited. "Captain, Mr. Chaffee is an able officer, one you can't afford to do without. An enlisted man you might spare, but not an officer."

147

"I'll agree to that," McCracken said.

"Well, I was an officer," Dandridge said. "Let me take his place, sir."

McCracken frowned. "Mr. Dandridge, you're a civilian, a correspondent. You're not required to perform a military task."

"I'm volunteering," Fields Dandridge said. "Captain, what I'm saying makes sense. You have to admit that."

"Yes," McCracken said, scrubbing the back of his neck, "it makes good sense." Dandridge had a strong point. But McCracken realized that if he let Dandridge accept a military assignment and harm came to him, his own military career would be forfeit; commanders took a jaundiced view of civilians engaging in army business. Even sutlers, like Janis, were not allowed to load a gun unless their lives were actually threatened. It was the army's function to make the frontier safe for civilians.

He reached his decision and bent over the desk to shake Fields Dandridge's hand. "You are a courier, Mr. Dandridge. Report here after the evening mess. I'll notify Mr. Chaffee of the change in plans."

"Thank you," Dandridge said. He turned to the door and then paused. "Do you have a map of the area? I may need it, sir."

"I think not," McCracken said easily. "I'll provide you with a guide. Mike Janis."

Dandridge looked relieved, smiled and left. McCracken looked after him for a time, then went back to his writing. When he finished the report, he sealed it in the dispatch case and carried it with him when he went out.

Mike Janis was at the cavalry stables when McCracken found him. The old man squinted and spat tobacco juice. "Bob, I want my daughter out of this place. She knows the country well enough to guide Dandridge, and I want her to go with him and stay at Fetterman. I mean it, Bob. If Gall storms this place, I want her long gone.

149

Gall's going to see that Crow blood and — "

"All right, Mike. If you want it that way," McCracken said. "Could you find Gall's camp for me, Mike?"

"Reckon," Janis admitted. "I'd want to do it alone though."

"Then find it for me," McCracken said. "I want to raid it."

"You do that and he'll come back at you with every man he's got."

"And I'll be waiting right here for him," McCracken said. "Mike, I've got to turn Gall's medicine against him, make him think that it's taboo to fight me." He paused to make a few mental calculations. "I figure I've got ten days. Marta and Dandridge can reach Fetterman by late tomorrow night. Brubaker will telegraph Platte Station right away; he'll have to because department will be on his back about opening the road for the settlers jammed there. It'll take the wagons four days to Fetterman and three more to here. Ten days, Mike, that's all I've got to give Gall a bad time of it."

Mike Janis scratched his head. "Admittin' that them artillery pieces of yours made a good impression on Gall, I'd still say that you'd never stop him once he got his wind up. You ain't got the men."

"Mike, I have confidence in my weapons and the men behind them. I've drilled this command for a year. I know what they can do."

"Sure you do, but don't get too cocksure, Bob. Gall's a brave man. One of the bravest. Was his medicine right, he'd come right down the muzzles of them guns and you know it."

McCracken sighed heavily and nodded. "Yes," he said, "I know it only too well. That's why it's so important to turn his medicine against him. I have the advantage when I can sit off at a distance, but, if and when he closes, I'd need infantry behind me. And I don't have them, just a troop of cavalry commanded by a man I can no longer rely on."

"You shouldn't be too hard on Glendennon," Janis said. "He took that scoldin' you gave him to heart, seems like."

"Maybe he did, but I'd never know for sure until the bullets started flying, and it's a poor time then to find out how wrong I was in thinking he'd straightened out."

"The trouble with you," Janis pointed out, "is that you judge a man too solid, either against you or for you. Men ain't like that, Bob. They can be hell an' gone in between somewhere." He turned and leaned against the stable wall. "When you want me to start my little sortie?"

"Tonight," McCracken said. "And, Mike, for God's sake, be careful."

"Will do," he said. "I like what hair I got growin' natural." He grinned and ambled away, his run-over boots scuffing the dirt in the stable yard.

McCracken stood quietly, reflecting

on what Mike Janis had said. The trouble with most frontier campaigns was that they were launched on a shoestring, held together with mud and spit, and died under the rock-heaving of public condemnation. A properly balanced organizational roster should have included at least six scouts, twice as many officers, and ended for all time this thin-spreading of man's forces.

McCracken knew he was assuming a lot of responsibility. But this was no longer a matter of personal failure. Brubaker would see to that. McCracken's failure would be the artillery's, and the next man who took up the fight would have to wipe out McCracken's defeat before he could even hope to begin re-establishing artillery's place in the army.

With this thought in mind, McCracken sagged against the wall, his face grave. His weapons were parked on the parade in front of him and he studied them. Beautiful machines, marvelously engineered, and nearly totally ignored as a first-line weapon of war. He could not blame Washington for a backward attitude concerning artillery; even during the Rebellion, cannon had been inaccurate, clumsy, and often dangerous. But these guns were different. He had to make them see that.

He returned to headquarters and threw open the windows to air the place out. Sergeant Karopsik came in and said, "Sir, I've been looking for you. Lieutenant Glendennon would like to speak with you."

"Is he outside now?"

"No, sir. In his quarters, sir. I can fetch him."

"All right," McCracken said and waited.

Lieutenant Harry Glendennon stepped brightly across the porch a few minutes later and came to attention just inside the door. He was all soldier now.

"Sir, I request permission to speak."

"Sit down," McCracken told him. He studied Glendennon carefully, not at all sure of this man. There was a small reminder of the fight marring Glendennon's cheekbone, a slight discoloration.

"Captain, I have a request to make," Glendennon said. "I feel that this is most important."

"Just what is your request?"

"I'd like to send my wife back to Fort Fetterman," he said quickly. "She can catch a stage there and return East." The young man's expression was unreadable, but McCracken suspected that resentment still simmered behind his bland face. Usually family trouble, even in the tightly knit circle of the army, was not discussed, yet Glendennon seemed willing to make it common gossip.

"You know I can't send her back," McCracken said.

"Lieutenant Chaffee is leaving tonight. I heard it from the sergeant major."

"Mr. Chaffee is not going," McCracken said. He got up and moved about the room. "Lieutenant, it seems that we got off to a bad start. Don't think I'm trying to pry into something personal, but can't you settle this between you and your wife?"

"No, sir," Glendennon said tonelessly.

"Perhaps I could speak to her."

"No, sir, the talking's done. We're no longer sharing the same quarters."

"I see. But this does not alter the situation, Lieutenant. I can't send her back with the detail leaving tonight. The trip will be a mounted one without wagons or ambulances. Not only that, it will be dangerous, with Gall's bucks roaming between here and Fort Fetterman." He smiled. "Mr. Glendennon, I don't think your wife is as tough as Marta Janis. She would slow them down too much; and I can't run the risk, for your wife's sake, and the sake of the mission."

Glendennon nodded. "I understand, but I had to try, sir." He moved his hands aimlessly. "You'll forgive me for speaking so bluntly, sir, but I don't think you'd ever be in this kind of a mess with a woman." He spoke too smoothly, which rang a small warning in McCracken's mind. This apparent contriteness did not fit into Glendennon's quick-triggered personality.

"What makes you think that?" he asked.

Glendennon smiled. "Because you're not at all like me, sir. I think I've proved to you that I'm little more than adequate."

"You made a bad mistake," McCracken said, "but that's no reason to bear a cross the rest of your life." This was, he felt, some kind of a game and the only way to learn the rules was to play it out to the end.

"Sheila will never forgive me," Glendennon said. He looked steadily at McCracken. "I love her. I can't help that, sir."

"We never can," McCracken said softly. "Glendennon, you're set on proving something to yourself, or maybe to her. And she'd have to

157

be here for you to do that. If you love her, fight for her."

"Sounds easy," he said. "Captain, it would be easy for you. I'm just not the type." He got up and stood there, rotating his kepi in his hand. "Perhaps if you did talk to her, after all . . ."

"All right," McCracken said. "But you'll have to beat your own drum, mister."

"I understand," Glendennon said. He saluted quite properly and hurried out. McCracken frowned. As an actor, Glendennon was a disappointment. In order to be convincing in one direction, Glendennon had overplayed his part, leaving McCracken broadly suspicious. He did not believe that the lieutenant loved his wife; and if he did, he had the peculiar ability to turn his emotions off and on at will.

McCracken stepped to the porch and cut across the parade corner. The sun was dipping, shooting a slanting heat over the post, but in another hour it would be gone and a cool wind would sweep the land.

He knocked on Sheila Glendennon's door, and she answered it so quickly that it almost seemed as though she had been waiting. She wore a simple cotton dress that from bodice to hip fitted like another layer of skin.

"Come in," she said, and stepped back. "You've avoided me, Bob."

"My primary function here," he said coolly, "is military, not social."

Her eyes grew round and she looked slant-eyed at him. "Ohhhh, you're in a fine mood." She turned away. "Did Harry come to you with his little problems?"

"Yes," McCracken said, "but it's a matter of opinion whether or not they're little."

"They're little to me," Sheila Glendennon said. "All of Harry's problems are little; he's not man enough to have a big problem."

"Do you really hate him so much?" McCracken asked.

"No," she said, facing him. "It takes a certain amount of respect to generate hate. I don't have any respect for Harry. Absolutely none."

"What you feel doesn't matter to me one way or another," McCracken said, "but it lowers the efficiency of an officer in my command, so I have to take an interest."

"Well," she said, smiling. "That was quite a speech. Are you going to send me back to Fort Fetterman?"

"No," he said, "not because I don't want to, but because it's impossible at this time. Patch this up with your husband, Mrs. Glendennon. Patch it up quick."

"Is that an order, Captain?"

"No. You're smart enough to listen to a suggestion."

She pursed her lips and regarded him solemnly. "Why don't you just send Harry away? I'm content to stay."

Her meaning was obvious, and blood filled McCracken's cheeks. Not the blood of embarrassment, but a quick-blooming anger. "What kind of a woman are you?"

"Heartless? I suppose you think that. But I have never liked the idea of being traded for a captain's bars. Brubaker's been hoping I'd involve you in an affair. That's been obvious, hasn't it?"

"It is now," McCracken said. "Is this something that your husband thought up?"

"Harry isn't smart enough to make an opportunity," she said. "he just has the small soul of an opportunist."

"That's not an answer," McCracken said.

"No," she agreed, "but you know without my telling you." She smiled thinly. "I was so tired of Harry that the idea seemed attractive to me. I'm not sorry it worked out this way."

"You're a lot of woman, Sheila. Under different circumstances, it might have been another kind of story between us. Glendennon may be what you say, small, but I wouldn't destroy him, or myself, for *any* woman."

"How can you destroy something that's already gone?" Sheila asked. "You're not being very realistic, Bob. That Colonel's out to get you, any way he can, and Harry was willing to help him. Why don't you just step on him now?"

"No, I can't do that," he said, turning to the door. "Try to patch this up between yourself and Glendennon."

"I'll think about it," she said, "but not very hard. You know, you're the kind of man who can just look at a woman and leave her bothered."

He went out without answering, took a deep breath, then started back across the parade ground. How like Brubaker to think of scandal as a weapon. McCracken recalled a major at Jefferson Barracks who had talked once too often to a sergeant's daughter while she secretly carried a corporal's child. There never had been a shred of proof, just talk, yet the major had had to resign. Glendennon's play-acting and apologetic manner suddenly assumed a substantial purpose, and McCracken felt relieved. Now that he knew the rules of the game, he could work for an ending slightly different from the one Glendennon and Brubaker had in mind.

The mess sergeant was calling the soldiers, and Sergeant Karopsik had a tray waiting in McCracken's office. When he had left, Marta Janis appeared, carrying a blanket roll and a rifle.

She set both in the corner, then said, "Was that your idea, sending Fields along?"

"He volunteered," McCracken said. He looked into her eyes and for an instant he thought he saw pleasure there, but then he decided that he had been mistaken. "You don't have to go if being with Dandridge bothers you, Marta."

She sat down and folded her hands. "It does bother me. I admit I care about him, but it's going nowhere, you understand? He'll get his story and then he'll be gone. I don't want to cry about it when he leaves."

"Well," McCracken said, "you have a point, but I guess you'll cry anyway."

"Sure," she admitted. "Only it will be easier if there's been nothing between us."

Fields Dandridge's step across the porch silenced her. He came inside and smiled at her, but she quickly looked down at her hands. Dandridge wore an old pair of trousers and a short, Texas brush jacket. He had done some jackknife work on his pistol holster, paring off the flap and the leather around hammer and trigger guard.

"Here are your dispatches," McCracken said, reaching into the desk drawer. He placed the flat leather container on the desk. "In there is an outline for the movements of wagons from Platte Station to Miles City. I'm sure Colonel Brubaker will approve. He has little choice with department riding his neck all the time. There is also a personal report for the colonel. Feel free to use the army's courier in sending out your own stuff, Fields. And make damned sure you send the facts, in which case you'll have to make sure that Brubaker doesn't get wind of it."

"I'll do that, Captain." He touched Marta Janis lightly on the shoulder, "Feel up to it, scout?"

"Don't call me that," she snapped.

Dandridge looked at McCracken, then again at Marta. "What do you want me to call you? Marta? Miss Janis? Or 'hey you'?" There was amusement in his voice and Marta gave way to it. She glanced at him and smiled briefly.

"We're killing time," she said, and picked up her blankets and rifle.

Captain McCracken went along and quietly saw that they were let out the main gate. He expected to see Mike Janis there, but the old man was conspicuously absent. An orderly brought up the horses, and Dandridge and Marta led them from the post. A full dark had settled and the blockhouses, only a few hundred yards away, were little more than smudges.

Marta was smart enough to know that Sioux eyes never left the post, so she mounted, motioning for Dandridge to follow suit. She led out at a walk and in the grass made almost no sound at all. Angling toward one of the blockhouses, she drew abreast of it, saw the startled faces of three soldiers, then cut toward the pass.

To Fields Dandridge, riding a length behind, the silence was almost a pain in his ears as he picked out every ink shadow, magnifying it to threatening proportions. His imagination, even though he tried to control it, placed a Sioux behind every bush.

For an hour they moved at a slow walk, and time began to saw at his nerves. The seat of his pants grew warm from the friction of constant swiveling in the saddle. Marta, by comparison, seemed unconcerned, although she paid strict attention to their surroundings.

Well into the pass, she vacated the more rocky ground, seeking instead the timbered slopes. This puzzled

Dandridge, and he would have liked to question her about it, for the probability of ambush here was too acute to ignore. She must have sensed his feeling because she slowed until she sided him, then leaned from the saddle and spoke softly to him.

"The Sioux have a fear of timber; they never spend the night in it if they can avoid it."

"But can they avoid it now?"

She shot a glance over her shoulder. "They're on the flats, on the other side of the post."

"Then let's get the hell out of here."

"We'll get well clear first," she said. "Gall will have a patrol in the pass. We don't want to run into them."

There was no more talk. Another hour dragged by while they threaded through the timber, keeping the pass to the right of them. Finally the country began to flatten into high plateaus, and Marta altered her direction to the right, breaking out at last on the Fort Fetterman road. Dandridge judged that

Runyon lay seven or eight miles behind them now, and when Marta urged her horse into a gallop, he was glad to follow suit.

After that it became a matter of riding, walking, and dismounting to ease the horses. He wanted to talk once in a while but she offered little opportunity. Every time he got ready to speak, she would mount and cut his impulse short.

He had a watch but the night was too dark to read it, so he guessed at the time, deciding that it was around three in the morning. Fatigue was beginning to send shooting aches into his back and legs, but he did not speak of them.

Marta left the trail quite suddenly, driving into the rocks until she found a small pocket, and there dismounted. She leaned against the horse for a moment, as though her legs were not quite able to support her, and when she stepped aside she bent to unkink stiffened muscles.

"You can talk now," she said, "as long as you don't yell."

"I wouldn't yell at you," Fields said. "We staying long?"

"Until dawn," she said. When she reached for her blankets, he brushed her hands aside and spread them out on the ground, then knelt and picked up all the small rocks underneath.

"I could use some coffee," he said, "but no fire for us, I guess."

"No fire." She sat down and lay back, her hands pillowed behind her head. "Good night."

"Good night? I thought you said we could talk."

She turned her head and peered through the night at him. "What's to talk about?"

"You," he said. "Let's start with you." He sat down beside her, close, and she inched away. He said, "I'm sorry. I didn't know you were afraid of me, Marta."

"Who's afraid?" She patted her holster. Cautiously she inched back, then retucked her hands behind her head. "You're a funny fellow, Fields."

"How's that?"

"You haven't got smart with me," Marta said frankly. "Maybe you play a pretty close game and take your time."

"It's no game, Marta. I've never met another girl like you." He picked up a handful of dirt and sifted it through his fingers. "I'm from Baltimore. You know where that is? Girls in Baltimore are not like girls here. I never could quite bring myself to trust one of them, but I'd trust you."

"Why?"

"Because you're honest. That's a wonderful quality in a woman, or a man. Ever been to Baltimore?" She shook her head. "Just a town. Big. Too big, maybe. You can get lost in a town like that. I don't mean the streets, but lose yourself. A man can grow up and never know what he is, and have no way of finding out."

"I don't believe it," she said.

"Everyone knows what they are. I know. Bob McCracken knows. My pop knows. How can you not know?"

"Life can get complicated," Dandridge said. "Have you ever had a lot of money?"

"I've got fifty-three dollars in the Wichita bank," Marta said.

"Multiply that times ten thousand and see how it changes everything."

"Yes," she said, raising up on an elbow. "It would."

Dandridge touched her lightly on the hand. "Have you ever thought what money would buy? A lot of money?"

"Sure," she admitted, "but most of the things I didn't need." She crossed her arms over her breasts and turned away from him. "Get some sleep, will you?"

"All right," he said, and lay down beside her. She raised up quickly and looked at him, then settled back again, stiff and tense. Dandridge waited a moment, then said, "This bother you, me being here?"

171

"I never had a man in my blankets before," she said. "I guess it's all right."

"You want me to move, I will," he said.

"Let's not jaw all night about it," she said. "If you don't mind, I guess I've got no complaint."

Dandridge settled on his back, using his hands for a pillow. Slowly, by degrees, the tension left Marta and her breathing deepened. The night was completely silent except for a very faint wind which whispered as it wove among the rocks. The horses stirred once, bringing him wide awake. Marta had turned over and the weight of her head on his arm made it ache, but he did not disturb her. He lay still, feeling the warmth of her against him, then he too slept.

The first light of dawn woke him and he stirred slightly. This brought Marta awake, and for a moment she lay there, trying to figure out what she was doing with her arms around a man.

172

She sat up abruptly. "I'm sorry," she said, and got hurriedly to her feet. She stretched, and stamped her feet, then crossed to the horses. He rolled her blankets and lashed them while she rummaged through her saddlebag. From a cloth-wrapped bundle she offered some cooked bacon and corn muffins. She kept her back to him, and when he put his hand on her shoulder, she moved away from it.

"Are you angry with me?" he asked.

"No," she said. "I'm angry with myself."

"What's there to be steamed up about?"

"You wouldn't understand," she said, and stepped into the saddle. "Time to be going."

Together they rode toward Fort Fetterman. She wouldn't talk although he tried several times to raise a conversation. The morning wore out and at noon they stopped at a bubbling creek to refill their canteens and water the horses.

Dandridge watched the land around them but saw nothing that reminded him of Sioux on the warpath. Through the afternoon they kept up the tedious rate of trot, walk, and dismount to lead, and it brought them to the palisade gates before sundown.

The officer of the day admitted them, then dispatched an orderly for Colonel Brubaker while the two went on to headquarters.

Brubaker came stomping in a few minutes later, took the dispatches and sat down behind his desk to read. Marta stirred restlessly while Dandridge lounged against the wall. Finally, Brubaker brushed the dispatches aside and pinned Dandridge with his glance. "Mr. Dandridge, I want the truth now. How well fortified does McCracken have Fort Runyon?"

"I would say that everything has been done," Dandridge said. "Captain McCracken's preparations have been extensive, Colonel. The captain has a strong weapon in light artillery."

"So he claims," Brubaker said. "But we don't win battles on claims, Mr. Dandridge. I have to examine this with a critical eye. McCracken has a lot of nerve, asking me to open the road on the strength of his preposterous artillery. I'll have to give this some serious thought, Mr. Dandridge. I'll let you know if I have a message to send back." He looked again at Dandridge. "A strong weapon, you say?"

"Very strong, Colonel. Too strong to ignore, officially or otherwise."

"Yes," Brubaker said. He got up and went to the door, calling the clerk. When the corporal appeared, Brubaker said, "Send the signal officer here, on the double, Wiggins."

"Aye, sir." Boots thumped briefly on the porch, then faded.

Brubaker came back to his desk. "Dandridge, you're from a fine family and seem to have a level head. I'll ask you for an opinion, unofficially. Do you think McCracken can hold Fort Runyon against Gall?"

"Well," Dandridge said, glancing at Marta, "you're asking me to prophesy, and I can't do that."

"But in view of the evidence," Brubaker prodded. "Mr. Dandridge, I know Bob McCracken. Knew him when he entered the army, over ten years ago. He's inclined to fanaticism when he gets his teeth into something. This time it's artillery. He's written articles for magazines, papers, and for anyone who'll read them." He went to the file and brought back a thick sheaf of letters. "nearly a hundred here. To Sheridan, Sherman, Cooke, Miles, Crook; every general who would read them. They've all been forwarded to me for recommendation. I turned all of them down. Any endorsement of mine would put my head on the block along with McCracken's."

"That may be true, Colonel." Dandridge said. "But since McCracken's willing to risk his career, he deserves backing."

"I suppose you're right there."

Brubaker sat down again and found a cigar. When he had it going, he said, "As soon as the signal officer . . . Ah, I think I hear him coming now." A captain entered the room and Brubaker indicated Marta Janis and Dandridge. "I believe you know these two, Collins. I have a message to go out immediately. And Mr. Dandridge may want to file his dispatches. I'll let you know when they're ready."

"Yes, sir," Captain Collins said, turning to the door.

"Oh, Captain," Brubaker said, "will you see that Miss Janis gets quarters?"

"Certainly," Collins said, and Marta went out with him.

"Close the door," Brubaker said, and after Dandridge shut it he offered the young man a drink of whisky and a good cigar. "You no doubt know that I've been strongly against artillery. Perhaps I should clarify my position. It's been my impression, through sad experience, mind you, that artillery slows down an army appreciably.

177

Campaigning against a hostile Indian force is one of striking movement. As a result I was particularly set against Bob McCracken's plan to turn my campaign into a personal proving ground." The colonel paused to gnaw his lip. "The decision to make now is whether McCracken can actually hold Fort Runyon against Gall. Mr. Dandridge, with the road open and wagons moving through, one massacre will finish me as far as the army is concerned. A man of my rank is not allowed to make a mistake."

"What can I say, sir? I have confidence in the man. Either you do or you don't."

"That's what it boils down to," Brubaker said. He got up and crossed to the window where he stared at the dark post. "Twenty-nine years in the army, Mr. Dandridge, and this is a difficult decision to make: whether to trust a man who stands for everything I hold alien."

"You'll gain by trusting him, sir."

Brubaker turned back, a smile on his lips. "Will I? Mr. Dandridge, when Washington gets a package too dangerous to handle, they look for a senior colonel to hand it to. That's how a general can stay clean enough to retire a hero. Man, look what happened to Carrington and Fort Kearney. No man could have cleaned up that mess at the time, but they had to do something. So they sacrificed Carrington to public opinion." He sighed and bit deep into his cigar. "Now it's happened to me. My orders are four sentences long, Mr. Dandridge. Open the road to the settlers. Put down the Sioux trouble. Reactivate Fort Runyon. Do all this without a full-scale war." He slapped his hands against his thighs. "That, Mr. Dandridge, is impossible."

"Looks like it's a matter of making a choice between two evils," Fields Dandridge said.

"Yes," Brubaker admitted. "That's why I'm going to send a telegram announcing that the road is open.

I'll choose Bob McCracken's way this time."

Dandridge finished his whisky then went out with his cigar.

As soon as the door closed, Colonel Truman Brubaker leaned back to reflect on this new turn of events. He had to admit that McCracken's plan had a certain degree of merit, especially since it gave Brubaker the chance to rid himself of an old enemy and at the same time keep his own record lily white.

He considered his conversation with Dandridge. Some nice touches there. Brubaker did not underestimate the importance of public opinion, and Dandridge, as correspondent of a widely read periodical, could wield power. Therefore, it was important that Brubaker have Dandridge's sympathy, and he was sure the talk had done its part in swaying the young man.

Drawing paper and pen to him, Brubaker composed his report, and after many pauses, he read the finished copy:

Fort Fetterman,
Wyoming Territory,
April 12, 1869.

To: Commanding Officer,
Department of Platte

Pursuant to a recent dispatch from Captain Robert McCracken, commanding Fort Runyon, I am of this date informed that Fort Runyon is now secure against hostile attack. On Captain McCracken's assurance, I respectfully request that civilian wagons be permitted to travel the surveyed road.

In a prior report I had occasion to sharply criticize Captain McCracken's military tactics as being theatrical and impractical in general field conditions. To date, nothing has occurred to alter that opinion, present situation included. It is my opinion that Captain McCracken's success, if any, at Fort Runyon, has been due to a relaxing of hostile activity, rather than an increase of military security.

Your most obedient servant,

Truman Brubaker
Col. Cav. Unattached,
Commanding Fort Fetterman.

Satisfied, Brubaker summoned the signal officer, and when he arrived, Brubaker handed him the message. "See that this is sent immediately."

"Yes, sir."

"Ah, Captain Collins, did Mr. Dandridge send his communiqué yet?"

"No, sir."

"When he does," Brubaker said, "I want to see the message before it's sent." He smiled thinly. "We wouldn't want Mr. Dandridge's youthful enthusiasm to stretch the truth now, would we?"

"No, sir. If Mr. Dandridge sends in a report, I'll bring it here."

"Thank you," Brubaker said. "That will be all, Captain."

After Collins went out, Brubaker's smile broadened. With one avenue of communication blocked, which was Fields Dandridge's, and the other wide open, which was Brubaker's, it would be a relatively simple matter to convince army brass that any failure here would be entirely McCracken's responsibility.

★ ★ ★

On leaving the colonel's office, Dandridge stood a moment on headquarters porch, then angled across the parade toward the guest quarters. But once there he paused, wondering what he would say when Marta Janis opened the door. He wondered what *she* would say, then decided there was only one way to find out.

He rapped solidly, with authority. He heard her step, and then Marta opened the door. She wore a robe and her bare feet poked out from the hem.

"I was going to take a bath," she said, then she remembered her manners

183

and stepped aside. "Come in, Fields."

"I won't stay long," he said. "But I didn't want any misunderstanding between us, Marta."

"There isn't," she said softly. "I made some coffee. Want a cup?"

"Thanks, I'd like it." He sat down in the only chair and she went to the small sheet-iron stove that served both for heat and cooking small meals. After she had poured coffee for them, she sat on the edge of the bunk, staring at her cup.

"I really wasn't angry at you, Fields. That's the truth."

"You were angry about something," Dandridge said. "Maybe it isn't important, Marta, but there ought not to be anything strained between us."

She glanced at him briefly. "I like you, Fields. It's just that I'd better not like you too much."

"What does that mean?"

"It means that you're from Baltimore and I'm from here. You couldn't live my way, and I don't know as I'd want to live yours."

This told him what he wanted to know, that she had been thinking of him in the way that he wanted her to think. He set his coffee cup aside and walked over to her, his hand light on her shoulder. "Marta, just accept me for what I am." He turned back to his coffee. "Brubaker's tune has changed, hasn't it?"

"He was lying," she said quickly. "That's what I think."

"So did I," he agreed. He drained his coffee, then moved away from the table. In passing, he touched her again. "Marta, don't fight me."

"Nothing good will ever come of it if we — " She stopped, realizing what she was about to reveal.

He lifted her gently to her feet and she moved close to him, her eyes never leaving his face. "I love you, Marta. Don't twist it or bend it around to anything but what it is."

His hand touched her face and then

he kissed her before turning to the door. She stood motionless, except for her eyes, which followed him.

"Good night," he said. "And remember what I said."

"It'll never work for us," she said.

"We'll see," he said, and let himself out.

She stood there for a moment, then gathered the cups and took them to the dresser. Her tub of water was growing cold and she shed her robe quickly, then stepped in, squatting down, her knees nearly to her chin. As she washed, her eyes began to film over, and then she put the soap and cloth down and let her head sag forward until her forehead touched her knees.

She sat that way while she cried in silence.

3

THE first wagons, when they were sighted from the Fort Fetterman palisade, were a surprise to Fields Dandridge. He had expected to see a caravan of rawhiders, poor and dispirited. Instead they presented a row of bobbing canvas, nearly twenty-five wagons, all good wagons, and when they drew near enough for him to make out the people, he saw that they were good too, not the down-and-outers he had anticipated. Farmers, merchants, even a gunsmith. There was money in this train, and a purpose behind this transplanting of civilization. Women sat on the high seats beside their men, and children laughed and called to each other.

Colonel Brubaker did not allow the wagons on the post, which had no room to park them. Instead, he sent Major Davis out to meet them, and the movers camped near the main gate, north of the road. That evening, Fields Dandridge went to Marta's quarters and together they left the post to visit the movers' camp.

Huge fires blossomed against the darkness as people moved about and a harmonica played while a man did a jig on a tailgate. Big Jim Durkee was the boss of the train, and his fire was easy to find. He turned out to be an average-looking man, which surprised Dandridge a little; but when Durkee made them sit down and eat, and presented his laughing friendliness to them, Dandridge understood why he had been named Big Jim.

Durkee had a wife and three small children. He introduced them and one of the little girls promptly climbed on Dandridge's lap and stared solemnly at him.

"Elsa, mind your manners," Mrs. Durkee said. "You got to excuse Elsa, Mr. Dandridge. She's shy, like my husband."

Durkee laughed. "My May's full of jokes." He squatted before the fire, his arms locked around his knees. "What kind of country is this we're going to? Good, like they say?"

"It's good," Marta said. "Farmers?"

"Most of us," Durkee said."They tell us it's wheat country."

"You got the summer heat for it," Marta said. "And winter snow for enough water."

Big Jim Durkee rubbed his hands together. He was a pleasant-faced man, and although Fields Dandridge had little liking for full beards he found Durkee's becoming. Instead of hiding his mouth and chin, it focused a man's attention on his eyes, which were bright and friendly. "A man can't ask for more," he said. "Ohio is about farmed out. Our place was old and it was small. A man's got to leave something to his kids. Can't keep cutting up an old place, one that's been cut six ways already." He waved his hands. "Why don't you folks move around?

189

Get acquainted?"

"Thanks," Dandridge said, and took Marta by the hand. For an instant, he thought she was going to pull away, but then she gave him a side glance and walked with him. They met the Petersons from Illinois. A big family, all strapping boys in bib overalls, with hand shakes like a saddle maker's vise. Beyond them were the Wilkensons from Iowa. Mr. Wilkenson was a dry-faced man who did not believe in smiling, but there was nothing standoffish about him; he merely lacked humor.

The Barlows had two wagons, a small covered rig and a huge farm wagon. Reese Barlow was a tall man, fifty some, who loved to talk. He insisted that Dandridge and Marta stay for coffee, and while they were seated before the fire a young woman came out of the covered wagon.

"She's the rest of the Barlow family," Reese Barlow said. "Meet my daughter, Ness."

She was tall, like her father, and

slender; some men would have said skinny at a first glance, but she was not, Dandridge noticed. Her hair was the color of fresh-shocked wheat. She had an open, friendly manner as she welcomed them. She sat down by Marta and spoke to Fields Dandridge. "What's the talk I hear about Indians?"

"More than talk," Dandridge said. "You'll have a cavalry escort clear through to Miles City."

"Now that's a real comfort," Reese Barlow said. He produced a corncob pipe and crushed tobacco in his palm. "Platte Station was sure a buzzin' with talk. Enough to scare a man half to death. Some Chief named Gall on the rampage." He paused to pull a burning fagot from the fire. After his pipe was going, he settled back. "A man don't want to spend his time fighting Indians."

"The army will do that for you," Dandridge said. "When we leave in the morning, we'll have an escort to Fort Runyon. There will be another there to take you on to your destination."

"Danged nice of the army," Reese Barlow said. His glance settled on Marta Janis and the ivory handled .44 she wore butt forward on her hip. "Never seen a woman packing a gun before. That customary out here?"

"It is if you were born here," Marta said. She got up and brushed off the seat of her pants. "Let's get back, Fields."

"All right," he said. "Glad to have met you people." He took Marta's arm and walked with her through the movers' camp.

Colonel Brubaker was standing by the main gate when they entered the post. "Babes in the wood," he said, nodding toward the camp. His jaws vised on his cigar. "Where do you figure on leaving them, Mr. Dandridge?"

"Well," Dandridge said, "Marta and I have talked it over and we figure that the first day's march will be the longest."

"She's returning with you?"

"Well — no, sir," Dandridge said. "Her father wants her to stay here, or go back to Platte Station."

"I see," Brubaker said. "Then I suggest that you make your camp this side of the pass. You can leave the wagons there and precede them into Runyon. Major Davis will be in charge of the cavalry I'm sending back with you."

"Yes, sir. Will that be all, Colonel?"

"I think so," he said. He turned away, his step crisp. Marta and Fields Dandridge watched him until he entered headquarters.

"He sure picked a peach to ramrod the cavalry," Marta Janis said with disgust. "Davis will take his bottles along and sing all night." She gave Dandridge a quick glance. "I bet Brubaker is sending Davis along *because* he's a boozer."

"We don't know that," Dandridge said, "but I'll watch him."

★ ★ ★

During the major run of his life, Robert McCracken had always taken great pains to disguise the fact that he was a chronic worrier; but daily his anxiety had increased to the point where a glass of whisky and a good cigar would no longer calm him. He spent a great deal of time on the wall and was forever asking the guards if they had seen any sign of Mike Janis. The man had been gone nearly three days on his mission to locate Chief Gall.

Yet the time had not been entirely wasted. Massive timbers had been shored against the wall's four corners and a heavy platform built there, complete with gun tackle and lashing. With an A-frame and the artillerymen's skill in disassembly, a fieldpiece was placed along the wall, and put together there, giving Fort Runyon a genuinely fortress-like appearance. With the guns elevated, McCracken could, if necessary, fire over his blockhouse and reinforce them if the fighting got too hot.

As he had many times in the past,

McCracken reviewed his preparations and, as always, they seemed complete and militarily sound; yet he knew from experience that a contest of arms would reveal many weaknesses, some that might prove disastrous.

Mike Janis's return was sudden and unexpected; the first inkling McCracken had was the guard's shout and the gate opening. Janis was afoot and looked considerably worn. He came on to headquarters with that peculiar, half-sideways shuffle of his and sat down in the lone chair.

"I need a drink," he said, and McCracken understandingly handed him the bottle.

Janis drank with a genuine thirst, then wiped his tear-filled eyes. "God," he said, "but that's strong!" He began to beat the dust from his frayed clothes, pausing once to have another drink. "A long walk," he said, "but I found what you wanted." He nodded toward the hills. "About sixteen miles, at a guess. There's a valley back there. Nice place, but swarmin' with Sioux lodges."

"How many?" McCracken asked.

Janis pursed his lips. "A hunnerd an' fifty, give or take a dozen." He squinted up at McCracken. "Lot of Sioux to take with one troop of cavalry. And it's a damn sure cinch you ain't goin' to get artillery back there."

"You're right," McCracken said, and went outside a moment. He spoke softly to a soldier and sent him toward Glendennon's quarters. Then McCracken came inside. "You had me worried, Mike. I thought you'd been done in."

"I'm more Injun than that. Heard from Fort Fetterman?"

"No. I didn't expect to, Mike."

"I still fret about it," Janis said. "Sometimes I wonder what's goin' to happen to my little girl." He looked steadily at McCracken. "What kind of a fella is Dandridge anyway, Bob? Is he like some I've known, just after her goods?"

"No," McCracken said flatly. "There's

honor in the man, Mike."

"That relieves my mind some," Janis said, "but then again it only adds to my worry. Maybe he's too good for her."

Glendennon's step across the porch brought Janis's talk to a halt. "Come in," McCracken said. "Stand at ease, Mr. Glendennon." He turned to his desk and sat on the corner. "Mike has located Gall's camp. We have about two and a half hours until sunset. Have your troop mounted on the parade in an hour. Ammunition double issue per man."

"Am I going into the field, sir? With one troop?"

"You are not going anywhere, Mr. Glendennon."

"Yes, sir. I thought it was like that."

"Mike will scout for me," McCracken said. "I'll command."

"I see," Glendennon said, a dismal note creeping into his voice.

McCracken caught this and said, "Understand that this is not a reprimand. It's just that I intend to stir Gall up a

197

bit before Dandridge returns and the wagons start through. The more of a licking Gall takes now, the softer he'll be when the big fight starts."

"Will that be all, sir?"

McCracken's nod dismissed him. After he had gone, Mike Janis said, "Now he took that right personal, didn't he?"

"I wasn't trying to hurt his feelings," McCracken said. "Mike, we've both seen a lot of men break. Some never get over it; but the ones who do pick themselves up and pull themselves together, and usually do a fair job of it."

"That's gospel," Janis said. "Ain't nothin' braver than a reformed coward." He got up slowly. "Well, if I got an hour, I mean to spend it sleepin'. Send someone around to shake me out."

When he had gone, McCracken gave his orders to Lieutenants Borgnine, Chaffee, and O'Fallon, then went to his own quarters, where he stripped to his underwear and changed into clothes already disgracefully worn by field duty. He was stuffing in his shirt tail when the door opened suddenly and Sheila Glendennon stepped inside.

"You ought to knock," McCracken said. He pulled up his suspenders, then buckled his pistol belt around his waist. "What do you want, Sheila?"

"What are you trying to do to Harry?" she asked. He gave her a wry glance and turned his back to her. This drove her anger near the surface and she stepped up to him, trying to pull him around. "Don't ignore me, Bob!"

"No," he said. "We mustn't ever ignore you, Sheila. That would really hurt you, wouldn't it?"

She whipped her hand across his face and slapped him solidly. McCracken's hair jumped but he continued to watch her steadily. She was instantly full of regret, putting her hands on his face gently, putting a soft caress in her voice. "Bob, I didn't mean that. Believe me, I'm sorry."

He turned, slipping away from her hands. "Leave me alone, Sheila. Go fight with your husband if you haven't anything better to do."

"He won't fight with me," she said. "I don't know what's got into him, Bob. The other night I stood there and called him everything I could think of, but he just sat and listened, then acted like he didn't care."

"He's getting smart," McCracken said. "He's ignoring you, Sheila."

"I don't like that, Bob. What have you been saying to him?"

"Nothing. I think you've said it."

"I hate him," she said. "Someday I think I'll kill him."

"Will you?" He raised an eyebrow. "Why? Because he no longer wants to have anything to do with you?" He turned away from her. "Harry's turned you down for one of Brubaker's promises, and your pride's hurt. What was there between you in the beginning, Sheila? There must have been something to make you marry him."

"A schoolgirl love," she said. "Or the uniform; he looked very dashing in blue and gold." She wiped a hand over her eyes. "Bob, I never wanted this to go to hell the way it has. It just happened, that's all." She sat down on the edge of his bunk. "Harry's changed. I hardly know him now. He came home a little while ago and said that you were taking his troop into the field to raid Gall's village. I don't know why he told me that, but it was hardly flattering that he would tell so obvious a lie."

"It wasn't a lie."

"What? That doesn't sound like you, glory-hunting. Now if it were Harry, it would make sense; he's like a little boy showing off by walking a high fence. I tolerated him for a long time, but now he acts like he's tolerating me. I don't much like that."

"I can believe that," McCracken said. "You couldn't live with a man you couldn't look down on. I guess that's why you married Harry Glendennon, because you felt superior to him."

201

"That's a rotten lie."

He picked up his hat and stepped to the door. "Better think about what I said, Sheila. Don't do something to Harry that you'll regret. He's already done enough to himself."

"Harry! How can you care about him after what he's been trying to do to you? You fool, I'm in love with *you*, not Harry."

"You're not in love with anyone," he said, "except maybe yourself."

She swore softly, and he closed the door, walking rapidly across the parade ground. Glendennon had his troop assembled and was waiting for McCracken. As the captain came up, Glendennon's glance went past him to his wife coming out of McCracken's quarters, walking toward her own. McCracken met Glendennon's eyes briefly and read a real hatred there.

"Mount informally," he said and stepped into the saddle. You too, Glendennon. I've decided to take you along." A trooper handed him a carbine and a belt full of ammunition. Mike Janis came from the stable yard, leading his horse. A mount was provided for Glendennon and he mounted without speaking.

The sun was down now, shooting long shadows across the parade. In another two hours, it would be grave-dark. Janis squinted at the sky, studying the packed clouds to the northeast.

"Weather makin'," he said. "That could be on our side if it rains."

At McCracken's signal the gate was opened and the troop filed from the post. Janis rode on McCracken's right, and he angled toward the pass as though the troop were moving back to Fort Fetterman. No one talked, yet every man understood that he was being watched carefully. McCracken held the troop to a walk and gradually they eased into the rocky land as darker night encroached.

After a time Janis said, "Let's walk a spell. Time to cut off the main trail."

They dismounted and led. Janis

moved out a few paces and found a narrow trail cutting between rock walls. Night became an obscuring veil and the going was slow, but the troopers held the noise down to a minimum. McCracken tried to maintain a sense of direction, but after another hour of this gave up completely and relied on Janis's instincts.

The wind was picking up sharply, lifting dust, scuffing it along, and finally there was the tangy flavor of rain. Each man donned his poncho as drops began to splatter, soon becoming a roaring drum.

Mike Janis went into the saddle and the troop followed him. With the rain noise helping to block out any sound they might make, their speed could be increased, and they rode boldly across the ruptured face of the land.

Rock eventually gave way to timber, and Janis found a trail leading them to a large valley. To the northeast lightning flashed and the drums of thunder rolled heavily. Janis made a circling motion with his hands, then swung off to the left, leading them for what seemed an interminable length of time to a rock overhang on the south end of the valley.

He pointed. "Horse herd below, Bob. Give you ideas?"

"You're reading my mind," McCracken said. "What's the land like around here?"

"Bluffs on two sides," Janis said. "There's a trail down back the way we came. A man'd have to lead his horse down it." He motioned with his hand. "This side's steep, but a man could make it afoot while someone else led the horses down the other side."

"Sounds good," McCracken admitted. He turned to the cavalry bugler. "Go back and ask Mr. Chaffee to come forward."

Janis grunted. "Don't you want Glendennon?"

"No," McCracken said. "Chaffee's in charge of the section, not Glendennon."

There was a wait while the bugler

walked back and everyone stood still, water pouring down their ponchos. Each man cradled his carbine against his side to keep it dry. Finally Chaffee splashed up. "Yes, sir?"

"Mr. Chaffee, Gall's horse herd is right below us in a box canyon. Janis tells me there's a trail around the other side, the way we came, where horse holders could lead the animals down. Have one of your sergeants move over there with the horses. The bulk of the command will remain here for a half-hour, and make sure you keep an eye on Glendennon." He turned to Janis. "Is that time enough for them to start down?"

"Twenty minutes would do it," Janis said. "I'll be with 'em."

"Good," McCracken said. "In twenty minutes I want your bugler to blow 'charge'. Have the horse holders discharge their pistols. We'll go down this slope afoot, scatter Gall's horses, then come to you and mount. With luck, we may drive them miles from here. Afoot, Gall will have real trouble blocking the pass when the wagons come through."

Chaffee chose seven men, including a sergeant and the young bugler. Harry Glendennon showed an obvious distaste for being placed in the second-in-command position of this detail but he kept his protests to himself. They brought up their horses, and with Mike Janis leading them, backtracked through the downpour to the narrow ladder-rung trail leading down to the valley basin.

Waiting was not easy, and the men moved about impatiently. When McCracken figured that fifteen minutes had gone by, he ordered the sergeant to deploy his men in a string along the rim. The rain began to slack off a bit, and McCracken wondered if it would be enough to keep most of the Sioux in their lodges. A few would be on guard, but those he could handle.

When the bugle blew and the first shots were fired, McCracken's first thought was that the sound was pitifully small against the drum of rain. But he saw a small commotion begin below in the main camp and chose that time to signal the command to go spinning and sliding down the steep slope. One of the troopers tumbled end over end, losing his carbine, but the main body had better luck. The trip was quick, even in the dark, and only a few met with mishaps, hitting rocks or losing control to go hell-a-tumbling to the bottom.

A hundred-foot slide on a rainy night held enough hazards, but once on the bottom, many new ones arose. The horses were rightly bunched, and a few shots into the air started them milling; flailing ponchos started them running. The Indian guards on the outer edges fired blindly amid a chorus of yells, but the horses were on the move and there was no stopping them. McCracken ran after the herd, shooting and yelling, while behind him, in a ragged line, the cavalry did their best imitation of whooping Indians.

Chaffee was careful not to lose contact, and when McCracken edged to the right, hoping to meet the sergeant with their horses, Chaffee followed with his men. McCracken realized that if Mike Janis had not been along, he would have missed the sergeant, but Janis was good at guessing and came to meet McCracken.

Each man vaulted into the saddle and stormed after the rampaging herd, now veering to the south of the village. This irritated McCracken. He had hoped that the horses would tear straight through Gall's camp, but luck deserted him. The Sioux were in an uproar, shooting, yelling, racing around in a frenzy of disorganization. McCracken did not bother to shoot in their direction. He led the troop past the village after the horses. McCracken recognized that such an attack could not be a complete success, and he had figured that a few of the more alert bucks would manage to catch up some of the fleeing horses for immediate pursuit. Signaling Wilson Chaffee, McCracken indicated that he wanted the rear covered, and the young lieutenant wheeled away with ten of the troop.

And none too soon, as over two dozen raging warriors stormed down, shooting and screeching. Chaffee met them, stirrup to stirrup, and they fired point-blank at each other. There was no attempt made to deploy and fight; they milled together, muzzles against breast, firing almost blindly.

Mike Janis suddenly pulled close to McCracken and pointed. On the rising rim to the east, muzzle flashes winked brightly and McCracken didn't need to ask who they were. He already understood that this was the rear guard that had been watching the pass.

"Keep the horses going," he shouted, and Janis forged ahead, accompanied by the bugler and two troopers. McCracken wheeled the rest of the command and rushed at the descending Sioux. Three to one poor odds, but that couldn't be helped. Close now, McCracken opened fire, feeling his revolver bang against his palm. Now and then a man went down, some of his own, and some of the Sioux. Then suddenly they were all jammed together and bullets flew haphazardly, men falling the same way. The Sioux charge had enough impetus to carry them through McCracken's puny force, which was a mistake, because the captain wheeled and started to drive them toward Chaffee, who fought with an almost unholy tenacity.

Joined at last, McCracken meant to rally Chaffee, but the man did not need it. He forged into the fight, pistol in one hand, saber in the other, and clung to his frightened, plunging horse with knee pressure alone. His blade whipped, cutting a swath through which he plunged on into the clear. But instead of remaining there, he wheeled his horse to re-enter the thickest part of the fighting. The Sioux were taking a licking, something they did not often do, and McCracken pressed them hard. His pistol was empty and with no time to reload, he fired the lone shot in his carbine, then used it as a flail, scattering men from their horses like a reaper with a scythe.

The Sioux had a bellyful of this; they easily tired of a fight when not winning. Whirling, they gathered, fired a few parting shots and ran for their camp.

"Let's get out of here," McCracken shouted, and then paused only long enough to pick up a half dozen downed men.

★ ★ ★

A short time later they stopped to blow their badly winded horses. Chaffee slid to the ground, cradling his left arm against him. He took off his rain-soaked neckerchief to bind it.

McCracken asked him, "Bad?" He nodded toward his wound.

"It will hold," Chaffee said.

McCracken looked about him. "Where the hell is Glendennon? Corporal, find that damn man."

There was a scurrying search, each man peering through the night at the next face. Someone called, "Here he is, sir." Then, "Better get forward, sir. The captain wants you."

Glendennon came up, and McCracken said, "There are a few words I want to say to you, but it can wait."

Chaffee said, "We'll have to walk back to Runyon, Captain. These horses won't be fit to mount for three days."

"Then we'll walk," McCracken said, turning as Mike Janis came up. "How long do you think we have before Gall can gather his horses?"

"Four days," Janis said. "Maybe five if the rain holds tomorrow."

"How far are we from the post?"

"Thirteen miles."

McCracken calculated. "A four-hour walk. We may make it by dawn." He turned to Chaffee. "Casualty report?"

One of the cavalry sergeants spoke

up. "Eight missing, sir. Six wounded."

"We don't want to leave anyone behind who's alive, Sergeant," McCracken said.

"No, sir. Shall I get up a detail?"

"Yes. Will you go with him, Mike?"

"I don't like the sound of that," Janis said, "but I'll go."

The detail formed quickly and the rest of the troop waited in soggy silence. Glendennon stood alone; he seemed to prefer solitude.

Janis and the detail returned, bearing a bleeding, groaning corporal. While the wounded man was made easy, Mike sided up. "Bob, you're making me plumb nervous hanging around here."

"I guess we're ready to move," McCracken said. He glanced at the man they had brought back. "None of the others alive?"

"No, sir. We found all but two. It was too blamed risky to look longer. What say we get out of here?"

McCracken had Chaffee assemble the troop. They fell into a loose marching formation, all eager to leave.

The rain continued, slacking, increasing, and toward morning dropping off to nothing more than a thick mist. But as dawn broke, it began again, hard this time. When the gates of Fort Runyon were sighted, every small creek was a raging flood.

Every man on the post was out to greet them as the men were dismissed on the parade. The horses were stabled by the artillerymen, an act that was unexpected by the cavalrymen but greatly appreciated. The wounded were carried to the supply building and made as comfortable as possible.

Captain McCracken went on to headquarters with Lieutenant Wilson Chaffee and once there, cracked the cork and each had two stiff ones from a water tumbler. McCracken produced cigars and the biting smoke drove some of the fatigue from them. The orderly came in and built a roaring fire, then left as they backed close to it to steam.

"Another mile," Chaffee said, "and I'd never have made it."

"It was worth a case of blisters," McCracken said. "We've salted Gall's tail and put him afoot." He smiled in spite of his fatigue. "I expect him to retaliate and when he does, we'll have a proper welcome prepared."

Lieutenant Borgnine came in, his face mirroring his relief.

"You can worry the hell out of a man, Captain," he said.

"I did what I started out to do," McCracken said. "Care for a drink, Gus?"

"No, thanks, sir." He glanced at Wilson Chaffee's blood-soaked sleeve. "Is that bad, Wilson?"

"Just a flesh wound," Chaffee said. "If you'll excuse me, sir, I'll go to my quarters."

As soon as Chaffee stepped outside, the captain began to talk to Borgnine. "I think now we can conduct our campaign with some hope of success." He leaned back in his chair. "Personally,

I detest officers who make it an occupation to sit back and stick pins in someone else's campaign, but I must add myself to this armchair corps. Gus, let's take a look at Fort Runyon and ask ourselves honestly why it has been so untenable."

"Poor location," Borgnine said.

"No worse than Phil Kearney, yet General Wessell held it, and defeated Red Cloud to boot." McCracken shook his head. "That's too obvious an excuse, Gus, and I'm leery of the easy ones. No, let's look deeper. Runyon has had two commanders and they both made the same mistake. They both tried to hold Runyon."

"Hell, I don't see how that can be a mistake."

"Gus, you're a better officer than that. What can you expect but failure when you sit on your butt and invite the enemy to attack? How can you win a campaign when you invite the enemy to a sniping party?" McCracken slapped his fist against his palm. "Strike, hunt them out, attack. I'm going to run Gall's rear into the ground. Chase the legs off of him. I'm going to hit him hard and while he's licking his wounds, I'm going to hit him again. Do you think I'm going to wait for the wagons to arrive so Gall can attack them? To hell with that. By the time the wagons start rolling, I'm going to have Gall's tribe worn down to a dozen squaws and a lame boy. And if there are more, at least they'll be coming at me, not those wagons." He got up and poured another drink for himself. "Go get some sleep, Gus."

★ ★ ★

On the porch, Chaffee took three deep breaths to steady himself. He felt a little ill from loss of blood, and whisky on an empty stomach made him strangely light-headed. He walked toward his quarters, unmindful of the rain and the dawn chill and his bone-deep aches. His arm throbbed painfully with every step, but the pain could be ignored.

His quarters were silent when he stepped inside, and he immediately began to strip off his rain-drenched gear. The arm gave him trouble, especially with his tunic and shirt, but he finally shed them, throwing them over the back of a chair. He built a fire and stood before the growing heat.

Behind him, the door opened and Harry Glendennon came in. He took off his cape and draped it over a chair back. "I could use a place to bunk," he said. "You wouldn't mind?"

"There's an empty bunk," Chaffee said. He was uncertain about what he should say.

"I've been asking myself why I made such an ass of myself," Glendennon said.

"The trouble with you is you're always fighting yourself."

He turned and looked at Chaffee. "I have to fight something." His glance dropped to Chaffee's arm, hanging limp and useless. "I wish I had that!"

Chaffee stared at him. "Hell, Glendennon, you're talking like a recruit at his first muster."

At any time before this the remark would have made him angry, but now he merely looked steadily at Chaffee. Finally he said, "If that's how I'm acting, I'm sorry."

He sat down on the other bunk and tugged off his boots, locking the toe of one against the heel of the other. Then he stripped off his soaked trousers and spoke to Chaffee again. "What am I going to do?"

"Do?" Chaffee shrugged. "You'll never be worth a damn until you straighten out your home life." He bit his lip. "Sorry, that wasn't my business. But I like the captain and I'm on his side. If you aren't, then you don't want to bunk in here with me."

"You think I'm against McCracken?"

"You sure as hell aren't for him," Chaffee said, and got into his bunk.

A moment later Glendennon lay back, staring at the ceiling.

* * *

A shawl helped keep the rain off Sheila Glendennon's head as she splashed across the parade to headquarters. Lieutenant Borgnine was just leaving, and she nearly rammed into him in her haste. He tipped his hat and spoke but she pushed past him into McCracken's office.

He looked at her sharply. "What is it, Sheila?"

"Harry left me," she said. "Just up and left."

"What do you want me to do, order him to bed with you? Or maybe take his place myself? That was the idea, wasn't it?"

She glared at him, then dropped her eyes. "Can I sit down?"

"Sure." McCracken placed his arms on the desk blotter. "I think it's about time we had a talk. Harry's not a good

221

officer or an honest man. I want to know why."

She studied her hands for a moment. "You already know the answer. I haven't been much of a wife to him, Bob. I talked too much, argued too much, and found too much fault with everything he did. Instead of Harry wearing the pants, I wore them. Now I'm sorry for it all. Whatever the mess he's in, I guess I did my share to put him there."

"Put him where?" McCracken asked flatly. "Sheila, does Brubaker have anything on Harry?"

"Enough. And I put the weapon in Brubaker's hands." He raised an eyebrow. "Harry and I had a fight. You know, one of those stupid things that start over nothing. To get even, Harry got drunk; he always gets drunk to get even. There was a cotillion; I didn't want him to go, drunk like that. But he did. He hit another officer. It could have ruined his career, except that Brubaker smoothed it over. But there was a price. And Harry's been paying it. She got to her feet quickly and went to the door, pausing there. "Bob, I'm ashamed and I want out. Please get me out!"

"Why? Because the game's lost its zest?" He waved his hand impatiently. "I'm not as stupid as Brubaker thinks, and I'm not going to be shot by your irate husband."

She slammed the door, and McCracken put his hands to his face and sat that way. He had enough trouble to satisfy any district commander, without having the frustrated urges of a passionate woman thrust on him. The rain continued to fall, drumming on the roof, making a distorted pattern on the windows. Finally he grew tired of watching and splashed across to his quarters. The room was damp but he did not bother to build a fire. Instead he lay on his lumpy bunk and thought of Fields Dandridge, somewhere on the trail from Fetterman.

* ★ ★ ★

Big Jim Durkee, who commanded the wagon train, was a man too gentle with his fellow man and animals to be a good driver, and for that reason the train made less than the time Dandridge had counted on. Big Jim was all for stopping the train when the rain began, but Major Davis, who detested discomfort of any sort, insisted that the march continue. He had small liking for any liquid not in bottles, and longed for a bed with a solid roof over it, and that was to be found only at Fort Runyon, still two and a half day's march away.

Fields Dandridge also had a couple of personal worries as he rode at the head of the column. Marta Janis had insisted on returning to Fort Runyon with the train, and Dandridge was at a loss as to how he would explain this to the old man. Marta had simply refused to stay at Fetterman, and that sounded like a pretty lame excuse even as Dandridge thought about it. And he wondered how he would tell Mike that he wanted to marry the girl; the old scout was suspicious of his motives already.

At each night camp, Reese Barlow had insisted that Marta and Dandridge eat at his fire. Now a wagon canvas had been stretched between wagon and two stout poles. This afforded shelter from the drizzling rain and protected the fire. Reese Barlow hunkered down with his pipe while Ness stirred a stew. Dandridge took off his hat and flailed it against his arms and legs to shed some of the water.

"A foul night," he said flatly.

"Tomorrow won't be much better judging from the sky," Barlow said. He looked at Marta. "You ought to get out of them wet duds, girl. Be takin' a chill if you don't."

Ness glanced at her father, handing him the spoon. "Watch that," she said, and took Marta by the arm. "I think my dresses will fit you."

225

"I don't need anything," Marta said quickly. She started to pull away from Ness's grip, but thought better of it and went around to the end of the wagon with her. Ness entered first, fumbling around in the dark.

"Don't dare to light a lantern," she said softly. "Silhouettes through the canvas." She patted a bundle covered with a blanket. "You can sit here."

Marta sat down, then said, "Really, you don't have to fuss for me."

"I'm not fussing," Ness said. She opened a trunk, rummaged through it, then held up petticoats and a heavy dress. "These will fit. Better get out of those wet clothes." When Marta still hesitated, Ness said, "Well, come on. We can't take all night."

Marta slipped quickly out of her soggy clothes, then dried with a towel that Ness provided. The petticoats came first, then the dress, and Marta turned so that Ness could lace up the back. When they came out of the wagon, Dandridge was talking to

Reese Barlow. He stopped when Marta came into the fire's light.

"What are you staring at?" she asked, and looked down at herself to see if something was wrong.

"You," Dandridge said. "I've never seen you in a dress before, Marta."

"I haven't owned a dress since I was twelve," she said, almost defensively. "I feel odd." She moved to the fire and stood with her hands spread. Ness took the stew off and served it. She made sure that the only place left to sit was by Fields Dandridge, and after a moment Marta took it. She ate in silence and when she was through, put the dish aside and stood up.

Ness said, "Stay here the night. The wagon's dry."

After a pause, Marta nodded. "I'll get my blankets." She turned and hurried off through the rain.

Looking after her, Reese Barlow said, "Strange girl. Don't figure her at all."

"Why don't you stop figuring people?" Ness asked. "You usually get everything wrong, Pa." Her glance touched Fields Dandridge. "Did you mind?"

"About putting her in a dress?" He shook his head and smiled. "You're a pretty observing woman, Ness. Thanks."

Her father looked from one to the other. "What in tarnation's goin' on here, anyway?"

"Nothing," Ness said as Marta came back with her bedroll. Dandridge stood up and said, "Think I'll go over to Major Davis's tent." He smiled at Marta. "Good night."

He left the Barlow fire and cut through the parked wagons. Major Davis had his tent pitched at the head of the trail where it could be struck first in the morning. He had a lantern going inside and Dandridge could see his shadow against the tent wall.

"Major?" he said, and stepped inside.

Davis had been nipping at the bottle; the lantern light showed a glisten in his eyes. "Sit down," Davis said. "A most miserable camp, Mr. Dandridge."

"Yes," Dandridge admitted. "I was

about to say good-bye to it, sir."

"What's this?" Davis stared for a moment.

"Time to leave," Dandridge said. "I'm riding ahead to Fort Runyon alone. Marta can stay with the train. If I leave quietly tonight, she won't know it until morning and then it will be too late to catch me."

"I see," Davis said. "Any particular reason for this?"

Dandridge shrugged. "I'll make better time alone." He stood up. "Any message you wish me to convey to Captain McCracken?"

"No," Davis said, after a moment's thought. "Tell him we'll be about a day behind you."

Dandridge stepped back into the drizzle and went immediately to the picket line, where he saddled his horse and made fast his poncho and blankets. He led the horse through the dark camp, through the sentries, and once clear, went into the cold saddle and struck out along the road.

The fact that he made noise did not concern him now; the rain would drown out the sound of his passage. The night was like the inside of a glove, a smothering black, and he could see no more than a few feet ahead.

Dandridge was not familiar with the ground he covered but he could make out the vague bends and twists of the road and in this way kept up his pace through the night. Morning found him bone weary and rain-soaked, but good miles from the movers' camp. He watched a gray and miserable dawn appear, dismounted for a brief rest, then went on at a much faster pace.

He rode with his carbine ready but saw nothing in the rocks on either side of the trail.

At last he mounted the last rise and looked down on Fort Runyon. The distance was short and his mission urgent so he rode the horse's last amount of strength out of him, approaching the main gate at a gallop.

They saw him coming and had the

gate open. Mike Janis was there, his old face screwed up with worry. "Damn, what does it take to scare you?" He grabbed Dandridge by the leg before he could swing down. "Bullin' through like that will only get you killed."

"You don't have to tell me," Dandridge said. McCracken came out of his quarters and hurried across the parade, splashing mud at every step. Giving his horse to one of the guards, Dandridge met him at headquarters and they went in together.

"You look like a wet coon," McCracken said. "Whisky?"

"I'd be obliged," Dandridge said, and sat down heavily. He took the glass and downed the shot quickly. After shaking his head, he said, "Major Davis and the wagons are one day out, Captain. Aside from the mud, everything's all right. Oh, I haven't told Mike, but Marta's coming back, too."

"Why didn't she come in with you, then?"

Dandridge shrugged. "I wanted to

make the ride alone, in case I ran into anything." He looked quickly at McCracken. "Hell, do you think I wanted to risk her neck? Now where in hell are all the Indians?"

McCracken told him about the raid and Dandridge wrote it all down, smiling often, pleased with the kind of story this was going to make in the Eastern papers. After folding his notes and placing them in an inner pocket, he helped himself to another drink, then sat loose in the chair.

"You're on the road to becoming famous," he said.

"Famous or dead," McCracken admitted. Long hours and a lot of worry were beginning to tell on him. New lines had formed around his eyes, and his forehead wore permanent creases now. "I suppose Brubaker stewed plenty."

"Between us," Dandridge said, "he says he has some hope for you."

"The hell!"

"So he says," Dandridge said. "But

don't you believe it. The campaign has been going sour on the old man, and he'd like to pull out of it with a clean record. Captain, he's going to lay the whole pile of chips on you. Better come up with a winner."

McCracken sighed and shook his head. "Fields, all I want to do is hold this fort and get the wagons through, and if I have to carry a campaign with eight breech-loading artillery pieces, then I'll try to do it." He rubbed his hands together. "You know, it's hell to be ambitious, Fields. Colors a man's judgement until he gets into the habit of stepping all over people."

"Is that what you do?"

"I've been guilty of it," McCracken said. "You know damn well I have. On the march out here I treated Gall like the blue-plate special at the Rathskeller; everything had to be according to the tactics. Well, I learned something on that raid the other night, playing like a cavalry officer. Fighting close is a rotten business; a man really doesn't know until he's done it. A lot of my theories went out the window and no one saw them go but me."

"I don't understand," Dandridge said frankly.

"I mean the idea I had about artillery having the ability to fight unsupported by any other arm, except for a little infantry backing and perhaps a cavalry flank." He shook his head slowly.

"That must have been hard to take," Dandridge said. "Captain, I wrote some copy on you and tried to sneak it out past Brubaker's nose. Didn't make it, though."

"You won't have to try that again," McCracken said. "I'll send a courier direct from here. I thought I could avoid thinning my ranks this way, but I can't. Get a dispatch ready and we'll put a rider on it tonight, Fields." He was silent for a moment, then he said, "You know, I was wrong to assume that artillery had the shock power of cavalry just because I could fire an explosive shell."

"Are you saying that you can't hold Fort Runyon?"

"I'll hold Runyon," McCracken said. "But I'm determined to do more than that, Fields. It's like pumping out a leaky boat; unless you patch up the hole it just fills up again. By the time I leave here, Gall will have to be whipped. Well, get some sleep. You can use it."

"At least ten hours of it," Dandridge admitted. He started for the door, then turned back. "Captain, thanks for sending me in Chaffee's place."

"Did you get anything settled?"

"Settled? No, but she doesn't shy away from me."

"Fields," McCracken said, "if this is too nosy, just tell me to shut my mouth, but what are you planning?"

"With Marta? Marrying her."

"Are you sure she'll mix?"

"She won't fit into Baltimore, if that's what you mean. I never thought for a minute that she would. But the West isn't always going to be like this.

It's going to grow towns, Captain. There's nothing in Baltimore that I want. Hell, a man could be governor out here if he set his mind to it."

"If you've decided not to go back," McCracken said, "then you'd better tell her about it. That might make a difference."

"I will," Dandridge said, and went out. McCracken could hear him speak to someone on the porch, then Mike Janis came in, pawing water from his beard.

"Damned rain," he said. "Get into a man's bones and aches. Didn't mind it so much when I was young. Pesters me now, though." He saw the whisky bottle and upped it. "I was standin' out there a spell, and I heard you and Dandridge talkin', Bob. I wasn't too surprised to hear that she's comin' back here. But, I wonder . . . Do you think I should butt in?"

"How do you want to see this go?"

"Don't know," Janis admitted. "Hard to decide, Bob. She's my daughter and

I want what's best for her, but dang it all, what's best?"

"Your decision," McCracken said.

"Uh-uh. It's hers." He motioned to the bottle. "Mind if I kill that? Helps drive the miseries from me." McCracken pushed it toward him and Janis drained it, then went into a fit of coughing. When he checked this, he said, "Smooth stuff. As I was sayin', that Injun blood makes her proddy, Bob. Gives her foolish notions that she ain't good enough for a white man. If beatin' it out of her was the answer, I'd flog her half to death, but that's no good. Talkin' ain't neither. Tried that. She's just got to see for herself, that's all."

"Then give her a chance," McCracken said.

"Huh?"

"Back off and let her have her head. You said it was up to her."

"Yup," Janis admitted, "that's what I said, but hang it all, my own medicine's damned bitter." He got up and stood idle. "What I come to tell you is that there's Sioux sign out there."

"Why the hell didn't you say so before?"

"Got sidetracked by new scent," Janis said. "Seen 'em about twenty minutes ago, bunchin' to the west of here."

"How many?"

Janis shrugged. "Ten, fifteen. Knowin' Sioux, I'd say they was five, six times that many. They got cute ways of not showin' their true numbers until they're ready to move in."

"Mounted?"

"Yup. Looks like we didn't shy all them horses like we figured. Likely some of the bucks was courtin' and had ten or fifteen ponies in the village by the lodges. I reckon they'll fight, Bob. They got their best bib and tucker on, and likely all the paint they could mix."

"Thanks," McCracken said, and followed Janis out, although he cut toward Borgnine's quarters. He found

238

the heavy-set officer asleep and woke him.

Borgnine grunted and stumbled to the water bucket. After splashing his face, he wiped, then threw down the towel. "That was a waste," he said. "I could have stepped outside and done the same thing. Something up, sir?"

"Gall," McCracken said. "Your section is fresh, Gus. Relieve Chaffee's men on the wall, then send Chaffee to my quarters."

"Yes, sir." When Borgnine had left, McCracken went two doors down to his own quarters. He paused only to get a spare box of pistol ammunition, then stepped on the porch in time to meet Lieutenant Chaffee.

"Looks like a party out there, sir," Chaffee said.

"Yes. Get five good men and send them out to the blockhouse. You take the north one. I'll have O'Fallon and five more men in the south one."

"Triangulation, sir?"

"Yes," McCracken said. "If they

239

come close enough." He paused then to look at the dreary post. Rain cascaded from the eaves and mud lay ankle deep on the parade. Artillery would be difficult to move now. The weight would bury the wheels and he doubted whether the horses could gain sufficient purchase, unless double harnessed. Then the thought occurred to him that perhaps Gall was thinking the same thing. "Well, we've made him mad," he said. "Let's hope that he's mad enough to bunch up good. I want that courier to have a clear run through to the telegraph at Laramie."

4

THE location of the blockhouses had been a scientific problem with Captain Robert McCracken, a mathematical calculation which he hoped would place him in a superior position against any attacking force. To anyone coming down the pass with the idea of storming Fort Runyon, the blockhouses offered a formidable defense, and to anyone attempting a raid from two other directions, the blockhouses could converge their fire, building an intense cone that the Indians could not penetrate.

That is, in theory.

But Robert McCracken no longer had too much faith in theory. His brief taste of Gall's fury had convinced him that Runyon might come under a direct, wall-climbing attack, and when that happened his artillery would be useless.

Climbing onto the wall, McCracken looked out at the bleak land. On the parade, Chaffee and O'Fallon were clearing the tunnel entrance, and with lighted lanterns they descended into the tube leading to the blockhouses. Borgnine's section was falling out to command the guns mounted high along the wall. Gun tackle was seized up taut to keep the rearing pieces from jumping off, and at last all was ready.

The Indians were boldly visible to McCracken, but they waited out there, offering no clue to their intention. Mike Janis slogged across the parade and came onto the wall by McCracken. "You think they're all gathered yet, Mike?"

"You want to guess, go ahead. It'd be as good as mine," Janis said. He glanced at the sky. The clouds were breaking, wind velocity had dropped off, no longer pushing the rain on a slant, and McCracken thought that the rain itself had slackened a bit.

"When they get settled good, we'll go

out and offer a fight," McCracken said. "Do they make you nervous sitting out there like that, Mike?"

Janis looked at him oddly, perhaps a little amused. "Well, if you ain't, I'll be nervous for you! You still figure you can fight 'em off with a bore swab and a Haines strap?" He popped a slice of cut plug into his mouth and vised it with his jaws. "By God, you do it and you're goin' to set some generals on their ears!"

McCracken stared against the mist-veiled hillside. The Sioux had dismounted and were crouched down, blanket-draped, patient and savage. Finally he turned, saying, "I'm going to my quarters. Call me if there's a change."

"Sure," Janis said dryly, and settled down to watch.

McCracken's room was damp and full of chill, so he built a fire in the sheet-iron stove and slowly the heat grew. The rain finally stopped, but the eaves dripped on until the shake roof lost its hold of water. Far out on the flats a shaft of sunlight broke through the scattering clouds; McCracken could see it from his front window, and as he watched, another shaft touched the earth, and still another until the day was bright. With the sun came a warming heat. In an hour steam rose from the soggy parade and the men patrolling the wall picked up the tempo of their step, feeling somewhat cheered by the prospect of fair weather.

McCracken lay down on his bunk and tried to sleep, but couldn't. His thoughts kept swinging to the Indians and Gall, who, he was certain now, hated him with a consuming intensity. McCracken had little liking for this task of pushing back one group of men to make room for another, but that was the way things were and he had his orders. He wondered if the settlers coming in with their wagons would even guess at the struggle that went on for them. Usually they did not; this was a past observation of

McCracken's. They came in with their plows and folksy ways, taking for granted that the land was theirs, even though it had been taken from the Indians with considerable bloodshed. And the government was on their side, assuming that the Indians had no rights and refusing to make treaties on the pretence that since the Indians were American born, citizens could not make treaties with their government.

Political rat race, McCracken decided, and turned his face to the wall. Some damn fool in Washington had sat behind a veil of expensive cigar smoke and decided that Gall would have to be sacrificed on the altar of westward expansion. And some eight dollar a week clerk had written up the order that moved men and got men killed. And didn't care very damn much either, McCracken thought.

He stayed in his quarters for nearly three hours, getting up only when an orderly crossed the parade and knocked on his door. "Come on in,"

McCracken said, and splashed water over his face.

"Mr. Janis would like to see you, sir."

"Any change in the Indians?"

"I wouldn't know about that, sir," the soldier said.

"All right," McCracken said. "Tell him I'll be along in a minute."

The soldier left and McCracken put on his hat and cape. The day had warmed considerably, but the rain had left a dampness in the air. He walked across the parade, pausing often to kick the mud from his boots.

From the wall, Mike Janis called, "Somethin' stewin' out there, Bob." He pointed and McCracken, once he was up the ladder, followed the general direction with his eyes. The Indians were clustered in a close knot but were preparing to mount their horses. Their numbers had swollen considerably since McCracken had last observed them; now there were nearly a hundred, and three quarters of them were mounted.

"Looks like they've been rounding up horses," McCracken said dismally. "We should have driven them farther, Mike."

"I allow we chased 'em far enough," Janis said. "Trouble is, Bob, you just can't scare off all a man's stock. A man's horse will come back to him. Leastways that's what I figure has happened here. There was a few mounts in the village and a few more wandered back. Then Gall sent men out to round up what they could." He took off his battered hat and scratched a mane of unruly hair. "Beats the devil out of me what they're doing up there. They ain't moved for hours, but now they're stirrin' over somethin'."

"I think it's time we riled them a little." McCracken said. He shouted to Sergeant Karopsik. "Get two runners out to the blockhouses, Sergeant. Tell O'Fallon and Chaffee that we're going to lay in a few rounds."

While Karopsik dashed off to detail the runners, McCracken turned to

Mike Janis. "Roust Dandridge and Glendennon, and don't waste time about it."

"Yup," Janis said, and jumped down, running across the parade.

McCracken used his field glasses to study Gall and his warriors. The Indians were still bunched, and McCracken decided that this was the time to determine his tactics, if Gall allowed any. McCracken studied the terrain carefully while several possibilities came to mind. He could allow Gall to block the pass, then lob artillery in there until they were scattered, but there was too much danger in that. Gall could take cover in the rocks and all the shells in McCracken's limbers would not get him out.

Then again, McCracken could lay down a line of fire and cut Gall off from access to the pass. This seemed a more realistic approach to the problem since the land was too rough to launch an attack from the rocks.

Both Dandridge and Glendennon

came quickly across the parade. They came up the ladder to the wall. McCracken said, "Mr. Glendennon, it will be necessary for me to take charge of your cavalry again. This sort of thing isn't to my liking, but I can see no alternative at the moment."

"Yes, sir," Glendennon said stiffly. "May I ask what you intend to do with them?"

McCracken motioned toward Chief Gall. "I suspect that his scouts have spotted the wagons coming and he hoped to attack them as they start down out of the pass. To do this he must wait there for them. I hope to disperse his force before they arrive." He looked carefully at Glendennon. "Now, Mr. Glendennon, will you kindly assemble your troop of cavalry. I want to charge Gall's position as soon as possible."

"Charge, sir?" Glendennon was impressed in spite of himself.

"It is, I believe, our only chance to save the wagons that are coming," McCracken said. "Gall will have to engage me and while he is doing that, I want Mr. Chaffee to lay in a few rounds to help cut him down to size."

"Gall will split his men," Dandridge said quickly. "You can't hope to hold that force with an under-strength troop, Captain."

"I realize that," McCracken said. "And neither can Chaffee lay down enough fire to keep Gall's entire force out of the pass. But I can draw their attention, make them come closer to the fort."

Glendennon turned and was calling his troop to order before he was halfway down the ladder.

"I'll get your horse saddled," Dandridge said.

The rest was waiting, the hardest part of any fight; McCracken wondered if Chief Gall found it so, too.

Glendennon's orders to his sergeant were brief and to the point, then McCracken hurried to his quarters for his pistol, saber, and ammunition belt.

Sheila Glendennon came out on her porch to investigate the commotion. She had not combed her hair and her eyes were puffy and red-rimmed. She saw McCracken run from his door and called, "Where are you going?"

McCracken paused to stare at her. "Gall's camped on the hills a few miles from the post. We're going to engage him."

"You're joking," she said.

"I haven't time to quibble with you," he snapped.

"You aren't joking," she said. "Bob, I don't want you to go."

"How touching," he said, and stepped past her. She reached out and took his arm, but he pushed her hand away. He went on across the parade where the troop was assembling. Men were missing and the sergeant quickly closed the gaps, bringing them into a slightly shrunken but compact unit. Fields Dandridge came from the stable, leading McCracken's horse. He waited for the captain at the gate.

From the palisade wall, Lieutenant Borgnine gave the signal that opened the gates. McCracken mounted and raised his hand. "Column of twos, Sergeant."

The troop rippled into motion with a clanking of sabers and rode out. McCracken, heading the column, bent low over the horse's neck and streaked for the pass. On the hill, Gall watched sharply and when he saw that McCracken was going to ride in his direction, he shouted once and the hostiles began to thunder toward the advancing cavalry.

Gall was a true general, although he wore no mustache wax; he knew exactly what to expect from the pony soldier. Another shout and a hand wave split his command, sending the newly formed segment in a circling movement.

McCracken, seeing Gall break off his forces, shot a glance toward the post with its artillery pieces poised and ready. Then suddenly less than two hundred yards separated him from the Sioux. He could see their savage paint and hear their wild shrieks as they bore down, having the advantage of high ground and numbers. The Indians began to shoot spasmodically, the puffs of powder smoke looking gray in the new sunlight. With pride McCracken noticed how disciplined the cavalrymen were; no shot was returned, nor did their line of charge break.

At a hundred yards he ordered them to halt and dismount. Afoot, with carbines hastily leveled, they fired in volley by squads, and even at the distance McCracken could see the shock that fire brought to the enemy's front ranks. The whole line quivered as though thrust through, and as the fire continued the wave broke like water striking an unyielding beach. Confusion, once planted, grew and at thirty yards the Sioux had become a milling mob.

Three of McCracken's men were hit. Several of the horses went down screaming, and two more men fell quietly over their carbines. McCracken held his ground and fired his pistol until it was empty, then took the one his sergeant handed him.

Nearly twenty-five of Gall's braves were scattered about, and nearly a third as many horses. And McCracken's fire ripped into the flanks, dropping more of Galls' prime fighters. But Robert McCracken remained a realist; he knew that he could not win this fight against such numbers.

Gall wheeled and regrouped out of rifle range, and this gave McCracken a chance to look to his wounded. A trooper was trying to stem the flow of blood from a hand shot through, while another stared stupidly at the white bones of his bullet-smashed leg. They seemed ready to suffer in silence and suddenly McCracken felt unworthy of such honor. He was sorry that he had led them to this untenable position. Maybe Sheila Glendennon was right; maybe he was showing off, trying to impress his men and the Sioux. Still, there had seemed no other way to save the wagon train . . .

While he stood there, waiting for the charge that would wipe him out, a rumble came to him and he cocked his head, unable to identify the sound or its source. Then one of the men pointed toward the pass and McCracken understood.

Just another mistake I'll have to pay for, he thought when he recognized the sounds of wagons and of cavalry. Major Davis had somehow made much better time than McCracken had calculated, and the cost of this premature arrival would be very high.

He understood now why Gall had regrouped; there must have been some exchange of signals from a lookout in the pass, signals that he had missed.

The waiting was over now. McCracken had to attack Gall before he could cut off the wagons at the pass. "Mount!" he shouted, and went into the saddle. The troop formed quickly and Gall recognized McCracken's intent. Wheeling, the cavalry charged into the Sioux guns, which began to pop irregularly.

★ ★ ★

These were the sounds Marta Janis first heard while riding halfway down the column near Major Davis's troop of jack-leg cavalry. At first she could not make it out, but when she topped the last rise and stared down, the entire valley was exposed to her view. Like diminutive toys, McCracken's cavalry wheeled and pivoted, crushing into the hostiles, trying to hold them back.

Major Davis's bugler sounded a broken-note charge, and the cavalry led the wagons off the pass at a gait too fast for safety. He wheeled his horse and cursed like a wild man, directing his anger at his sergeant for not keeping the troop properly bunched. Davis was not much of a soldier, but in the recesses of his mind lurked sound tactics; and he knew that the Indians would try to hit the wagons with one swoop, carry through, and crush his cavalry with ease.

But once moving, he was committed to a rapid trip off the pass. The wagons seemed to gain momentum as they rocked down the rutted trail, threatening to overrun the teams and spill. He brought the cavalry out of the way, racing along to one side as wagons roared past, banging, sliding, canvas tops flapping, passengers trying to hang on.

Davis rode his frightened horse in choppy circles. The Indians could be distinctly heard now, and he noticed that the hot fight McCracken had stirred up was dead and that Gall's warriors were coming toward him.

★ ★ ★

McCracken's troop was tattered and bleeding as they mounted the remaining horses. Their fight was spent; no more than half their original strength remained.

Suddenly the corners of Fort Runyon became a bright blossom of flame, and an instant later a flat-voiced boom was heard. This was followed by an ear-breaking explosion and a column of earth headed skyward, taking a few of Gall's braves with it. Davis was not sure who was more terrified, the movers of the Sioux. Several teams bolted completely, and some men jumped to save themselves, only to be set upon by the Sioux.

The first artillery volley was followed in rapid succession by more, this time from the two blockhouses. McCracken drove his jaded and cut-down troop toward the wagons, stringing his men out to add to the weaponed front exposed to the hostiles.

He had little time for observation. The whole column was a confusion of flying earth and sounds and voices trying to make themselves heard. Davis's bugler was sounding recall and McCracken wondered, recall from what?

Amid the confusion, McCracken rode like a madman, driving his horse to the last limit of speed. He did not seem aware of the fight now and he cursed himself for not being more detached, more observant. The Indians were turning back, harried by the barrage Chaffee, O'Fallon, and Borgnine were laying down. Then the barrage lifted and it took McCracken a moment to understand why. The first of the wagons were past the blockhouses and the artillery were unable to fire from that quarter. A lone gun kept banging away from the post, but even that ceased fire and the entire column made it to the gates on the last bit of steam they had left.

McCracken was inside the gate before he realized it. The shooting had stopped, the rumble of wagons had died, all replaced by a silence that almost made his head ache. He flung off. Around him was a confusion of wagons and men, and then Lieutenant

Borgnine was striding up.

McCracken hurriedly climbed the wall, his field glasses scanning the field of battle. Apparently the wagons had all reached the fort safely except two abandoned earlier by fearful drivers. Now those drivers were dead and Gall's bucks paraded around them, lifting hair, hacking off hands and feet.

His cavalry had suffered the most casualties, but had taken the greatest toll in enemy dead. Gall would long remember the troop that had knelt at McCracken's command and fired in volley, ignoring the threat of Sioux might.

There were his men to recall; McCracken sent Karopsik on this errand. McCracken left the movers to Mike Janis, who went among them bringing some organization out of the confusion.

McCracken thought of his dead scattered in the field and felt that there was something almost obscene about their just lying there, to be gathered by a burying detail when it became convenient.

"Sergeant!" McCracken sent his call over the post, then waited until Karopsik came running up. "Sergeant, have two wagons hitched and two squads of riflemen ready in ten minutes. We'll gather up the fallen."

Sergeant Karopsik was not in the habit of questioning an order, but he swallowed hard on this one.

"There's Indians out there, sir."

"I'm aware of that," McCracken said.

"Yes, sir." Karopsik ran off, calling for a corporal.

While McCracken waited, Mike Janis sided up, his wrinkled face grave. "What's this about pickin' up your men, Bob?"

"You don't think it wise?"

"Danged tootin' I don't!" He mopped a hand across his face. "Bob, you got a hole cut in you out there and you're still bleedin' from it. Ain't you lost enough men?" He jerked his thumb toward the land beyond. "Gall's liable to come at you and where would you be with wagons and foot sojers?"

"I don't want to discuss it," McCracken said flatly.

"Stubborn idiot," Janis said, and walked away.

The wagons were ready; a corporal was forming two squads taken from the gun crews. Dismounted formations were not to their liking, but they pulled themselves into twin rows and prepared to march out.

With the wagons in the lead, McCracken took his detail from the post. He could see a remnant of Gall's band on a far ridge and wondered if they would attack him. The wagons stopped often, and McCracken had to stand there while some lifeless soldier was cord-wood stacked in the wagon box. Mentally he crossed them off his roster; Haggerty, Cummins, Delaney, Snow, Showers . . .

The wagons moved on and the detail stood about, rifles ready, guarding those few who were already in the wagons. McCracken kept watching the hill crests, expecting a charge, but none came. He supposed that Gall's heart was as heavy as his own, for the Sioux had their own dead, their own grief.

Within an hour McCracken's command was again together, the living and the dead, and he turned his group toward the palisade gates.

Headquarters was McCracken's haven, the hub from which all the spokes of command radiated; and once in his office, he had Major Davis, Lieutenant Borgnine, and Fields Dandridge summoned. While the hubbub of the post went on, McCracken looked at these men with mingled feelings.

There were, in Major Davis's attitude, shards of regret, for he was in the position many officers had been in after a campaign: a little sorry they had not acted differently.

About Fields Dandridge there hung a strange aura of peace, of a man who had observed a high-stake game and its winning; his prize waited outside, a tired girl who he hoped had decided something important during the lonely miles to Fort Runyon.

"Major Davis," McCracken said, "may I welcome you to Fort Runyon? That was a brilliant charge down the pass, Major. It's too bad you couldn't have expended some of that energy toward the hostiles."

"I resent your insinuation, sir," Davis said.

"I'm sure you do," McCracken said. "Mr. Borgnine, I'm placing Lieutenant Chaffee in command of a full troop of cavalry. Replace the men lost from Major Davis's troop."

"Just a moment . . . " Davis began, but McCracken's blank stare cut him off.

"Major, do you think that decision wrong?" McCracken asked easily. "Well, speak up."

"No," Davis said dismally. "You're in command here. My brevet commission doesn't cover arguing with post commanders."

"Thank you," McCracken said. "You're dismissed. Dandridge, you stay." He answered Davis's and Borgnine's salutes and waited until the door closed. "Brubaker could have sent me anyone but him and made me a lot happier."

"Is there something wrong with Davis?" Dandridge asked, his smile wide.

"Major Davis," McCracken said evenly, "is what we call a marginal soldier. He has had several commands, none of them completely unsatisfactory, but nothing outstanding. This is unfortunate, in a way, because the frontier demands more than adequacy in a soldier; it demands the best." He glanced at Dandridge. "I believe you know what I mean, Fields."

"I do, sir."

"Mr. Dandridge, I'm going to write up a report and send it along to Brubaker, but like always, I'm faced by a problem in communication. If I had a large post, I could easily detail a squad of men as couriers and have them ride in relays, but that is both impractical and impossible. The ride to Laramie will be both fast and hazardous, and I can't expect a courier to come right back if I send him." He paused a moment. "Mr. Dandridge, do you feel up to a ride in to Fetterman with the colonel's dispatches?"

"Certainly," Dandridge said.

"Be sure and listen carefully to what Brubaker has to say."

"I'll sure do that. But what about my story? I want my paper to know the truth, not Brubaker's watered down version."

"I've considered that too," McCracken said. "I plan on sending one courier a week to Laramie and he can telegraph to Washington anything you want to say. That way, your reports go out and I don't thin out my command so fast." McCracken ripped the wrapper from a cigar and struck a match on the under side of his desk. "We put up a hell of a fight today, Fields, and it didn't decide a damn thing. Gall's hurt, and so are we and our only consolation is that he's hurt worse. But this isn't over; in fact, it's just begun."

"Gall's going to think his medicine went sour," Dandridge said, "if you keep on hitting him this way." He grinned. "But my medicine's fine, Captain. Those wagons brought back what I wanted."

The door opened and the orderly thrust his head inside.

"A young lady to see you, Captain."

"I'm busy now," McCracken said. "Later."

The orderly shook his head. "Sorry, sir. You'd better see her."

"I've got to be going, anyway," Dandridge said. "Dispatch of my own to write." He stepped out an instant before a young woman stepped in. The orderly closed the door and the young woman leaned her back against it. Her expression was pinched and her complexion chalky. She held her left arm against her body and supported it with her right hand.

"You've got to help me, Captain," she said, her voice tight with control.

"If I can," McCracken said. "You're with the wagons?"

"I'm Ness Barlow," she said. "I think I've broken my arm."

Her casualness jarred him more than anything, and he hurried over to her, helping her into a chair. He was not a doctor but he had seen enough fractures to know that she had one, a clean break between wrist and elbow.

"How did this happen? Coming down the pass?"

She nodded. "A lurch threw me backward off the seat and into the wagon bed. My weight came down on the arm. It was pinned against a heavy trunk." She looked at him. "My father's busy; I didn't want to bother him with it."

"We have no doctor here," McCracken said gravely. "Miss Barlow, will you trust me to set it?"

"Yes," she said. "If that's the only way."

He looked around his bare office, then decided to take her to his quarters. She went out with him, holding her breath, for every step jarred her arm and sent pain shooting through her. The post was a beehive of activity; every man there seemed frantic with energy, straightening out the wagons into a park, reorganizing. The palisade guard had been doubled and a constant lookout was maintained along the wall.

Once inside his quarters, McCracken motioned for her to sit on the bed, then went to his pine dresser and brought out a whisky bottle and glass. "Have you ever been drunk?"

"No," she said. "Are you going to get me drunk?"

"It'll be better," he said. "This won't be fun for either of us."

"All right," she said, and took the glass. She drank it down, choking as tears streamed from her eyes.

He poured some more into the glass and gave it to her. She held it for a moment, looking at him. "I read a penny dreadful once where a heroine was in a man's room and he gave her wine. Am I going to meet the same dangers?"

"Not this time," McCracken said with some amusement. "Down that."

She obeyed, with less strangling this time. She was not accustomed to this, and the effects were already becoming apparent. It was difficult for her to focus her eyes and there was a slur in her speech when she spoke.

"Oh, dear," she said. "I'm dizzy."

"One more then," McCracken said. He poured, but withheld the glass, giving the whisky a chance to work without making her sick. "Where are you from, Miss Barlow?"

"A farm. We're all from farms, Captain." She swayed a little, and McCracken, afraid that she might fall and further injure her arm, sat down beside her and steadied her with his

270

arm. "Wh — what are you doin'?" She looked at him with a glassy stare. "I guess you're all right all right. But you got to watch out for some men." She paused and placed a finger against her cheek. "I got light hair. You got red hair. Say, if it wasn't all right all right, would a baby have red hair or light hair?"

"Lie back," McCracken said, pushing her gently.

"Oh my," she said loudly, "it isn't all right all right."

He reached for the whisky, intending to give it to her, but decided that he needed it worse than she did. He shook his head and felt carefully along her arm for the break. "Do you feel that?" he asked.

"Sure, but I don't care. I'm a sinned woman, I guess, an' poor pa don't even own a shotgun." She looked at him but her eyes were blurred. He grasped her wrist and gave a sharp tug, feeling the bones go into place. Ness Barlow's back arched like a hickory bow for an instant and she sucked in a great, agonized lungful of air, then fainted.

Quickly, McCracken lashed together a splint out of stove kindling, ripping up a towel to bind it with. He worked for several minutes, then stood up, wiping the sweat from his face.

Ness lay quietly and McCracken covered her with a blanket, then went out, walking directly toward the wagon park where the settlers milled. He asked at a half dozen wagons and finally found Reese Barlow looking for his girl.

"I'm Barlow," the man said, answering McCracken's question. "But I got a lost daughter. About as tall as a hay fork, with a shock of yaller hair."

"I know where she is," McCracken said. "She's had an accident. I have her in my quarters."

"Accident?" Barlow grunted and scratched his head. "What the blue blazes you talkin' about?"

"She broke her arm coming off the pass," McCracken told him. "I just set it. She's in my quarters, but I'm afraid she's in no condition to be moved. I had to get her drunk to set it without hurting her too much."

"Drunk!" Barlow was more shocked at this than the broken arm. "My little girl drunk? Scandalous, that's what it is! I'll go to her." He started off but McCracken pulled him back.

"When she feels better you can go to her, Barlow. Right now, I'd say to leave her alone. I'll get Marta Janis to look after her."

"Well," Barlow said, "as long as there's a female with her. I raised her proper, I did. Nobody's to fool with her, you understand?"

McCracken was nearing the end of his patience, but he checked his first impulse to say what was on his mind. "I'll keep you informed," he said. "Now, if you'll excuse me, I have things to do."

Unpleasant things, although he did not say so. Honesty drove him to construct a mathematically exact report for Colonel Brubaker; and even as he wrote, McCracken realized how powerful a weapon he was placing in the colonel's hands. The attack he had led had, for all practical purposes, been a cavalry maneuver; and Brubaker would dangle this fact like a ripe plum under the noses of Washington generals, striking a further blow against the practicability of artillery in the field. Brubaker would completely ignore the fact that cavalry had been used to drive the hostiles into the maws of permanent emplacements, which was a standard working tactic in any army.

McCracken wondered what he could do, hitch up his limbers and chase Gall with the battery? He laughed, then sobered, for the thought, wild as it first seemed, had some merit. Of course he could not take the whole battery, but one gun without limber was no more awkward than a wagon. He finished his report and sealed it, making a mental note to investigate the idea further.

He found Marta when he found

Fields Dandridge. Mike Janis was with them, hunkered down with his chew of tobacco and his solitary thoughts. He looked up at McCracken, then said, "Squat. You been doin' too much chasin' about. Had a dog that-a-way once. Never could sit still. Always chasin' somethin' or other."

"No time for sitting," McCracken said. "Marta, how well do you know Ness Barlow?"

"Good enough, I guess," Marta said. "Something the matter?"

"She hurt herself," McCracken said. "I've got her in my quarters now, but I'd be obliged if you'd move in with her until she's on her feet."

"I'll be glad to," she said. "But where are you going to bunk?"

"Well," McCracken said, "I'm not sure. Maybe with Borgnine and Chaffee."

"Can't," Dandridge said. "Major Davis moved in with them. He pulled a little rank on Harry Glendennon, and he had to move back with his woman."

"I guess I can sleep at headquarters," McCracken said.

"I — ah — moved the women and kids in there," Dandridge said. "Well, hell, Captain, I had to put them some place! Your office is now in the old guardhouse. Sergeant Karopsik says he's going to get the roof fixed in case it rains some more."

McCracken flapped his arms against his sides. "Do you suppose there's room with the horses, Fields?"

"I filled up the stable myself," Mike Janis said. "Davis's troop took all the room."

Dandridge smiled. "Captain, you want me to get a couple of men and dig you a cave?"

"You go to blazes," McCracken said, and walked away. He went on the wall for a look around and saw that Chief Gall was still dog-eyeing Fort Runyon. Coming up to Lieutenant Wilson Chaffee, McCracken said, "That's a dismal view if I ever saw one."

"You'd think he'd have a bellyful,"

Chaffee said. "He took a hell of a licking from your cavalry."

"You were lobbing a few in there yourself," McCracken said. "I'd give a year's pay to know what's going on in that mind of his right now. Gall's smart, and I'm trying not to forget it, even for a minute."

"He nearly had the wagons," Chaffee said. "When that fool major forged ahead, I thought they were done for."

"Mr. Chaffee," McCracken said, his eyes slightly amused, "be careful of what you say or you may never become a first lieutenant."

He turned then and went down the ladder. The rest of the day was spent moving about the parade, talking to the settlers, telling them that there was no real trouble with the Indians, just a minor disturbance that would be cleared up in a few days so they could all leave. McCracken did not deceive himself that anyone believed him, but he kept on saying the things they all wanted to hear, and they lapped up his words like divine gospel.

The evening meal was an hour late and McCracken, then went to his new office in the abandoned guardhouse, where he found Sergeant Karopsik.

"Sergeant, can you find me a place to sleep tonight?"

"Sleep, sir?"

"Yes, Sergeant. I do sleep when I get the chance. I've lost my quarters to an injured woman."

"Well," Karopsik said, "I'd be glad to lose my quarters to any woman." He saw that the humor was lost on McCracken. "Yes, sir. Right away, sir." He grabbed his hat and hurried out.

McCracken turned his head as someone approached the door, then got up to answer the knock. When he opened the door, Marta Janis was standing there. She said, "Sorry to bother you, Bob, but Ness Barlow's awake now and wants to see you."

"Wait for me," McCracken said, and quickly scooped up his hat.

The night was quiet and there were stars and a soft wind. A few lights brightened windows, and along the palisade wall guards walked their posts with measured tread. Marta said, "Who would think there were Indians out there?"

"I'd think it," McCracken said. "What's the matter with Miss Barlow?"

"Nothing," Marta said frankly. "I just think you need a woman's company. Since I don't trust Sheila Glendennon, I suggest Ness." She looked at him, a trace of smile on her lips. "Are you mad?"

"No," he said.

"Well, come on then. Ness is still a little furry tongued from all that poison you made her drink."

She went ahead of him into his quarters. A lamp was lighted, spreading a small puddle of light by the bedside. Ness Barlow was now wearing a cotton nightgown so loose fitting that it almost seemed to swallow her up. Her arm was in a sling and a pillow had been placed across her stomach to rest it on.

"Hello, doctor, or should I say bartender?" There were still lines of pain around her eyes and lips, and she kept her left hand clenched. The effects of the whisky could still be seen in the redness of her eyes.

"I've got to see pop," Marta said, and left in a hurry.

McCracken stood with his hat in his hand as the door slammed. Ness Barlow said, "Please sit down. I was hoping you'd come back. I've taken your bed, haven't I?"

"I'll bunk with one of the lieutenants," McCracken said. He sat down feeling a little embarrassed, and this bothered him. "Feeling a little creaky?"

"Not half as bad as I did when I walked in your office," she said. "You're not a bad doctor."

"Better bartender," he admitted.

"I got pretty drunk, didn't I?"

"Good and quick."

"Did I babble?"

"No," McCracken said, too quickly.

"Oh," she said. "I did. I'm sorry."

"Look," McCracken said, "we're talking ourselves into a hole. You didn't say anything to be ashamed of, so let's forget it."

"Yes, sir." She smiled. "That's me, always making a fuss over nothing."

"Like broken arms?" He shook his head. "I've seen grown men cry over less than that. Are you this pioneer stock I've heard so much about?"

"Just a farm girl," she said. "People are only brave in retrospect, Captain. Take my father. To hear him tell it, the modern generation has gone to rack and ruin. Now his mother was a woman. She could plow two acres of bottom land from sunup until noon, have a baby by two o'clock, and bake four pies and eight loaves of bread by supper time. But I understand. I'll seem the same way with my own children. And they'll be the same with theirs." She paused and smiled again. "You see, there I go blabbing some more."

"Go ahead," McCracken said. "I like to hear it."

She cocked her head to one side and regarded him a moment. "What are you like, Captain?"

"My name's Bob."

"Then what are you like, Bob? I don't mean now. I mean when you were a boy. Did you ever push over outhouses on Halloween? Or swipe the banker's buggy to take your girl for a ride?"

"I was a quiet type," McCracken said. "Although I did paint Mrs. McTavish's horse a bright yellow when I was a wee lad. It seemed to keep the flies off him."

She laughed and said, "Why yellow? I'd think blue or green would have been better."

He shook his head. "Yellow was all I had, and I'm a man who does the best with what he has at hand."

"I'm sure of that," Ness said. "Look what you did with a couple of glasses of whisky and some kindling."

She closed her eyes for a moment as though a stab of pain drove everything else from her mind. Finally she relaxed slightly, although the tension remained around her lips. "Did you know I was scared to death coming off the pass. I thought the Indians were going to reach the wagons."

"I had a moment when I wasn't sure myself," McCracken admitted. He got up then and stood by the bed, looking down at her. "Get some sleep now, Ness. I'll drop in later on."

"Can I consider that a promise?"

"A promise," he said, and went out.

Marta Janis was returning as he stepped off the porch. He took her arm. "Let her sleep for a while, Marta. Walk with me, I want to talk to you."

She fell into step beside him. "Oh? What about, Bob?"

"How about you and Fields? Is everything settled between you?"

"I love him, if that's what you mean."

"Not exactly," McCracken said. "You

had some foolish notions, Marta."

"They weren't foolish to me," she said softly. "You don't understand, Bob. I can't have him the way a white woman can, married." He started to speak but she shook her head. "Let me finish, Bob. He doesn't know this and there's no way I can tell him. So I'll do like my mother did. I'll go to him and perhaps bear his child, but that's all, Bob. That's absolutely all. I'd ruin him if I married him, and when he grew to hate me for what I'd done, I'd have ruined myself."

He wanted to shake her, to slap her, to tell her about the plans Fields Dandridge had for staying on the frontier, but he knew that he could not speak of these things; this was Dandridge's business and the young man would resent an intrusion. Then there was Marta; she would suspect such a move as something designed to soften her own hurt, and rebel against it out of pride. McCracken sighed. "You're wrong, Marta. So wrong."

★ ★ ★

Within twenty-four hours, McCracken discovered that the movers had made themselves at home; neat rows of tents crowded the parade and in the evening cook fires glowed brightly. McCracken found time to worry about Fields Dandridge and the courier he had sent east over a trail guaranteed as sound by Mike Janis. Yet worry was not the answer and McCracken knew it.

In the early evening he had Chaffee ready his section, and at dark he left the post with twenty men and one artillery piece, minus limber, which if pulled by fresh horses could go anywhere a buggy could go, and just as fast. Mike Janis served as scout.

The rest of the night was spent in finding Gall's village, which the chief had moved after that first raid. At dawn, McCracken threw two rounds of explosives into the camp, turning it into pandemonium. Then he limbered and raced back to the fort before the

Sioux could run them down in wrathful vengenance.

But retaliate they did, with a dawn raiding party two days later. McCracken was waiting for them; the walls bristled with rifles and after a heated exchange of small-arms fire, the Sioux withdrew, leaving four of their own dead, and Sergeant Karopsik nursing a bullet-pierced arm.

That night McCracken took Lieutenant Borgnine into the field with twenty men and one gun. Again Mike Janis led the detail, although he considered this kind of warfare sheer insanity. By midnight, they found a Sioux encampment, although it was not Gall's main camp, and McCracken fired three rounds into it before departing.

Instead of returning to the post, he camped in the hills for a day and a half, then made a night march back to Fort Runyon.

Again the Sioux struck back, spending more of their ammunition and leaving a corporal in the second section dead.

McCracken considered himself fortunate for not having more casualties, but he did not take to the field for three and a half days. He figured that after two quick raids, Gall would be wearing his men out guarding the camp, and that was what McCracken wanted — for them to shoot up their ammunition and wear themselves bone-poor.

Still, there was the matter of his own ammunition. He had plenty of artillery shells, but the small-arms ammunition was running low. He summoned Major Davis to his office one evening, and said, "Major, according to the colonel's dispatch, which you carried when you arrived, I see that one of the wagons contains small-arms ammunition."

"That is true," Davis said.

"I trust that you sorted it properly in the hut?"

"Indeed. The very next day."

"I need to draw from it now," McCracken said. "These raid have all but depleted my ration. How many rounds have we, Mr. Davis?"

"Mister?"

McCracken frowned, then looked at Davis. "Your rank is only brevet, and I have no need for a brevet major in my organization. Unless I am incorrectly informed, you are still a lieutenant carrying a brevet rank left over from the Civil War."

"Yes, sir. That's true."

"With that settled, let's get back to the ammunition. How many rounds do we have?"

"Ten rounds," Davis said smoothly. "Ten rounds per man."

There was a moment of stunned incredulity when McCracken could only stare, then he grew wildly angry. "Was this the damned colonel's way of getting me?"

Davis smiled thinly. "No, sir. I have the honor of being responsible."

A coolness returned to McCracken then. "Mr. Davis, you're due for a court-martial."

"Am I?" He shook his head. "With ten rounds of ammunition per man, you'll never get out of here to prefer charges." He stood up, his expression stiff. "I would have been a captain now if you hadn't had me relieved of my command. Do you remember? It was in '62, and I can give you the month and the day if you like."

"It took you all this time to get even? You're not very efficient, Mr. Davis. And you were never very sober." He stopped and took a deep breath in order to control himself. "I suppose that is the reason Brubaker sent you here, to be a stone around my neck."

"I thought it at the time," Davis said. "You don't understand me, Captain. You never did. I made a mistake and you ruined me. So I drink too much. What was that to you? I ask you, what did it matter to you? Hell, I wasn't in your damned company! Did you have to report me?"

"Being drunk and an officer at the same time is bad," McCracken said. "I don't give a damn for you, Davis, but I cared for the men you could have killed. Now I want to know about the ammunition. Brubaker stated that he sent a hundred rounds per man. Did you change that?"

"Yes," Davis said. "Very simple. I just told the orderly sergeant that there had been a mistake."

The urge to hit this man was so strong that McCracken could scarcely restrain himself. He sat with the palms of his hands flat on the desk to keep them steady. "You are willing to sacrifice every man on this post to get back at me? Mr. Davis, I'm going to see you shot for this!"

"After you fight a campaign without ammunition?" He shook his head. "I always wanted to be a soldier; did you know that? That was my ambition, to be a good soldier. Only I was a poor one. Some men could do something else, admit they failed, but I couldn't. A man has to do something, either go down in fame or infamy, and fame is impossible for me. I think we'll all die out here and I don't give a damn. I guess Booth felt like that when he shot Lincoln. We'll all be dead and we'll all be heroes and they'll look at you, then at me, and never be able to tell us apart."

"Better get out of here," McCracken said. "Go on, Davis. Just get the hell out and leave me alone."

The silence was thick after Brevet Major Elwood Davis left. McCracken remained motionless, feeling for the first time the actual terrible weight of his predicament. He had automatically counted on a renewed supply of ammunition from Colonel Brubaker. Such a thing was standard operation procedure in the army; it went without saying, without thought.

Ten rounds per man!

McCracken pulled the duty roster around and read the casualty list. *God, had he actually lost half his command?* He put his face in his hands and sat that way for a time.

If ever Truman Brubaker needed verbal ammunition to oust him, he had it in the damning record of half a command lost. There was no hope now. Even if he were to kill or put on the run every Sioux in Dakota he could never rise above this dismal record. As he had feared all along, his plans were not good enough; he had led his command to failure.

Sergeant Karopsik came into the office, took one look at McCracken and said, "Something the matter, sir?"

"Huh? No. Nothing's the matter. Just tired, Sergeant."

"Maybe a cup of coffee," Karopsik suggested. "Lieutenant Chaffee's got some in his quarters."

"I don't think — " McCracken stopped. "Thank you, Sergeant. That might help at that." After Karopsik left, he blew out the lamp and went out, crossing to Chaffee's quarters.

Wilson Chaffee answered McCracken's knock. "Captain," he said, "you came at the right time. Want some hot coffee?"

"What I could really use is some

whisky," McCracken told him. Then he decided to tell Chaffee about the ammunition shortage. As Chaffee sat motionless, his eyes growing increasingly angry, McCracken told him about Major Davis and his treachery.

When McCracken finished, Chaffee said, "I drew sixty round per man when we left Fetterman; thirty for revolving pistols." He made a few mental calculations. "I'd say that we've expended roughly three quarters of that so far, but I'd have to make an individual count before I could say definitely."

"Well, it must be very low," McCracken said, "which means that we'll not be able to sustain a close range attack or carry on the fight to Gall. I suggest that you make a head count in the morning, Wilson. We should know exactly where we stand, to the cartridge."

"Why wait until morning?" Chaffee asked. He stood up and put on his hat and cape. "This won't take long."

"I'd as soon you waited," McCracken said. "I don't want this spread around the command."

"Sir, they'll never know my purpose. I'll make it sound like a junior officer giving a typically stupid order." He left and McCracken followed him outside.

Chaffee disappeared into the shadows, and McCracken walked slowly toward his own quarters. Lamplight framed the window and he knew that Ness Barlow was still there. He had urged her to stay on for a time since he had been away from the post so much. It was oddly comforting to think of her there.

He knocked, and she let him in, smiling. "I'm so glad you came. I was getting lonesome," she said. She noticed his serious expression. "You look like the end of the world's approaching. Are things that bad?"

"No," he lied. "Not bad at all." He scraped his hand across his unshaven face, then said, "Mind if I stoke up the fire and shave?"

"Of course not. Your things are still

in the drawer. I snooped."

He looked at her quickly, then laughed. "Talk to me, Ness. You're just what I need." He fed some kindling into the sheet-iron stove and in a moment had it roaring. Ness watched as McCracken lathered his face and broke out his straight razor, stropping it carefully. While he was shaving, the front door opened and Reese Barlow came in, stopping when he saw McCracken shaving.

"Well, now, ain't this right homey?" he said. "Ness, I come to take you back to the wagon."

"There's no need for that," McCracken said, studying Barlow in the mirror. "But it's up to Ness. She's welcome here."

"Seems like you're going out of your way to be obligin'," Barlow said.

McCracken toweled his face dry before turning around. "What would you do?" He rebuttoned his collar and straightened his neckerchief. "Who is in charge of the wagons?"

"Big Jim Durkee," Barlow said. "Ain't no trouble, is there? We been mindin' our own business, and the army's been stayin' away from our women. We like it that way."

"Pa!" Ness said, embarrassed.

"I'm a man who speaks his mind," Barlow said flatly. "You married, Captain?"

"No," McCracken said. "Thanks for the use of the stove, Ness." He went outside before Barlow could say any more. The older man looked disgusted; he liked to be heard out even when he really had nothing to say.

Ness said, "You didn't have to act that way, Pa. Captain McCracken's been real nice."

"Huh!" Barlow said. "A lot you know. Anything in pants looks nice when you want to get married." He sat down, his wrinkled face showing his displeasure. "I try to tell you to be careful, Ness. But you just don't listen to me at all."

"People get tired of listening," she

said. "Pa, you talk so much you make a person's ears hurt. After a while it gets so I can shut out the sound of you talking."

"Well," Barlow said, "I see there's no thanks from you for what I've done." He got up and tramped around the room. "How come you went to him for help anyway? I'm your pa, ain't I? Ain't it fittin' you'd come to me with your hurts?"

"You just don't understand," Ness said.

"What's there to understand?" Barlow asked. "Ness, it puts a man in a dunderment just tryin' to figure you. You're twenty-three and ain't married yet. That's enough to worry your old pa. Seems like the men I pick for you just ain't good enough." He jammed his hands deep in his overall pockets and stood that way.

"You hurt me, Ness. You really did, turnin' from me to that captain when you was hurt."

"I had to, Pa. Believe me, I had to."

Reese Barlow shook his head slowly. "Don't understand it. I'd do what was right for you, Ness. Lord knows I would."

"There are times," she said softly, "when a girl wants to do for herself, even if it's wrong. Now would you mind leaving, Pa?"

"Sure," he said, edging toward the door. "I know when I ain't wanted."

"Why do you say that?" she almost shouted. "Why do you have to twist everything around and be a martyr all the time?" Then she turned her back to him. "Just go, Pa. Go on."

"Sure," he said again, and went out.

★ ★ ★

When McCracken left his quarters, he started toward headquarters and was intercepted by Wilson Chaffee. "I've been looking everywhere for you, sir." He took a notebook from his hip pocket. "I've made an accurate survey;

every man counted his cartridges. We have less than twenty per man."

"You didn't let on to the men, did you?"

"No," Chaffee said, "but they think I've lost my mind, wanting a cartridge count." He laughed a bit uneasily. "What do we do, sir?"

"I haven't decided," McCracken said. "A meeting of officers first, I guess. Go about quietly and round them up. Get Glendennon and Mike Janis too. Assemble in my office in fifteen minutes."

Returning to his office, McCracken put a match to the desk lamp and then sat down to wait. Major Elwood Davis was the first to arrive and he stepped boldly through the doorway as though challenging McCracken to question his right.

"Sit down," McCracken said. "I wondered if you'd have nerve enough to show up, Davis."

"You underestimate me," Davis said. "But then you always did that, underestimate everything. Maybe that helped make your own limited powers seem greater."

"To hell with your philosophy," McCracken said. "If you can't keep your mouth shut, get out." Borgnine, O'Fallon and Chaffee were coming across the porch. McCracken was surprised to find them appearing older than he remembered; he had been too preoccupied since their arrival at Runyon to look really closely at his officers, and now he saw that trouble had taken its toll.

In a few moments, Mike Janis and Harry Glendennon came in. "Close the door," McCracken said to Glendennon. When this was done, McCracken leaned back in his chair and looked at each of them, sorting out his thoughts. His first impulse was to expose Davis for what he was, but he decided against that. He had already confined in Wilson Chaffee and now he regretted this, because at such a time each of them needed the utmost confidence in each other.

"Gentlemen," he said, "it has come to my attention that a grave error has been made by a party or parties now unknown. The ammunition normally expected has failed to arrive with the cavalry relief commanded by Mr. Davis." This set up the buzz he had expected, and he calmed it with a lifted hand. "This is neither the time nor the place to fix blame. The problem confronting us is: what are we going to do with only twenty rounds per man?"

"Good Lord!" Borgnine exploded. "How could such a bungle have happened, sir?"

"We don't care how. It just did." He glanced at Davis and found him sitting ramrod straight in his chair.

"The responsibility is mine," Davis said. "I must assume it." He wanted to be exposed, McCracken realized. Even shame was better than anonymity.

"There's no need for that," McCracken said smoothly. "Mr. Davis, I'm convinced, beyond a shadow of a doubt, that you are blameless. I'm sure these gentlemen will take my word for it."

They all nodded, and this left Davis petulant and lip-biting.

Mike Janis shifted his tobacco to the other cheek and said, "Bob, seems like a good man could sneak past them Injuns and tell Brubaker what's happened. Then maybe a relief column could get through to us."

"Wagons alone would never make it," Borgnine said dismally.

"But cavalry could," Glendennon said. "Captain, I request permission to go and bring back a troop." He saw the resistance in McCracken's eyes and stepped past Chaffee to come closer to the desk. "Captain, I'm sure I could get through. Instead of bringing the ammunition in a wagon, a troop of Fort Fetterman cavalry could pack double, even triple the normal allotment. Gall must be running low on shells too, and the minute he sees a lone wagon, he'll know what it must contain and he'll hit it with everything he's got. And with our present ammunition situation, we could hardly go out to fight him off or divert him."

"The boy's makin' sense," Mike Janis said. "Sounds good, Bob."

"It sounds risky," McCracken said. "I don't like it."

"No one asked you to like it," Janis said bluntly. "Twenty rounds per man ain't much, Bob, and from the looks of things, Gall's goin' to hit you as regular as payday for quite a spell."

"All right," McCracken said finally. "Get ready to leave, Harry. And pick a fast horse."

"Yes, sir," Glendennon said. "Any dispatches, sir?"

"No," McCracken said. "Just tell the colonel the situation here." From Glendennon's expression, McCracken knew that he had not fooled this officer. By not carrying dispatches, there was nothing to fall into Gall's hands should Glendennon not make it. Gall had been to the white man's school and could read English, and should he find out there was only twenty rounds of ammunition per man . . .

"Mr. Glendennon," McCracken said, "I dislike asking this in public, but I would like to know why you're so anxious to take charge of this detail?"

"I wish to leave; not because of the situation here, I am no longer frightened by the prospect of dying. My reasons are quite personal, Captain. I'm sure you understand."

"I think so," McCracken said. "That will be all."

The group broke up, all except Elwood Davis, who remained behind. "Someday," Davis said softly, "I think I'll kill you."

"Even that may go sour on you," McCracken said. He got up slowly and came around his desk. "I'm not going to try to understand you, Davis; it would be a waste of my time to try. But I'll tell you something and you'd better believe it. You're not going down in history as anything good or bad, because I'm going to save you for a court-martial and an official firing squad."

Davis stared for a moment, then hurried out, stumbling off the porch. McCracken waited a moment then stepped out to stand in the black shadows to the right of the door.

Glendennon finally appeared, leading a fast horse. McCracken walked to the main gate and offered his hand briefly, "Good luck and ride like hell."

"I'll do that, sir," Glendennon said, stepping into the saddle.

At McCracken's signal, the gate was cracked and Harry Glendennon eased through. Then McCracken climbed the ramp ladder to observe the lieutenant's journey to the pass. But the night was dark and a hundred yards from the post both horse and rider disappeared.

McCracken mentally tried to measure Glendennon's chances of getting through alive. He knew that Gall no longer had a ring of warriors around the fort. The night raids had taught Gall the wisdom of staying in his own back yard, which had been McCracken's hope when he began his harassing tactics.

The danger lay in the fact that Harry Glendennon was not much of a plainsman; he would make mistakes and never know that he had made them until it was too late. McCracken decided, though, that he could trust Glendennon; the man was at last forgetting personal ambition and settling down to being a good officer.

McCracken went down the ladder and stood idle for a moment, then decided he ought to walk through the movers' camp, to give them confidence. This struck him as humorous, the army giving someone confidence. If they only knew the situation, the whole army and the navy thrown in wouldn't ease their minds.

Or mine, McCracken thought.

He walked easily around the camp, then started down the gap between the double rows of tents and makeshift shelters parked wagons, with the dotting fires and jams of people close-huddled as if packing themselves together could push aside the trouble outside the walls.

He stopped to start a conversation with Big Jim Durkee and Barlow came up, butting in without hesitation.

"Anythin' goin' on here I should know about?"

Big Jim Durkee gave him a look that would have scalded a coon, but Barlow ignored it; hooking his thumbs in his overall bib, he rocked back and forth on his heels.

"I was about to speak of the firearms among you people," McCracken said, drawing on his patience. "Mr. Durkee tells me that all of you have shotguns and a rifle or two."

"That is kee-rect," Barlow said. "We're peaceful people, Captain, not given to violence. Farmers mostly, although there's a few tradesmen among us. A butcher, a hardware man. Alex Rettig is a gunsmith, but you'll not find — "

"Gunsmith?" McCracken asked. "Where is this man?"

"I'll show you," Durkee said. "Good night, Barlow."

"Huh!" Barlow said. "I know what end the tail's on. Don't have to hit me with a spade to tell me I ain't wanted." He stomped away, the image of outrage.

"Rettig is parked on the other side of the camp," Durkee said, and led the way over dropped tongues and dying campfires. He found Rettig's wagon without trouble, a huge Conestoga that had been converted to half-wooden sides. Rettig was asleep in the bed, a string-thin German-Swiss, who had to fumble for his thick glasses before he could identify either Durkee or McCracken.

"Vas is it?" he said, peering out. "Ach, *Herr* Durkee. Vat a time to be vaking a man up."

"Mr. Rettig," McCracken said, "I understand that you're a gunsmith."

"Ya. From Zurich. Eferbody carries guns here. I should haf a lot of business."

"Maybe I can give you some now," McCracken said. "Mr. Rettig, do you have any way of making a bullet mold?"

"Ya, I can make a mold. Vat caliber?"

"Forty-five," McCracken said. "I'll bring you a bullet for a pattern, although it can vary somewhat without suffering any. Can you set up to make it tonight?"

"Tonight?" Rettig adjusted his glasses. "*Mein* lathe, she has to be set up lefel . . . "

"I'll have the men to do that for you," McCracken said. "Mr. Rettig, do you have any silk or paper?"

"*Nein*, but I think I know vat you want. I haf saltpeter vich vill make any paper burn. Dat iss no problem, *Hauptmann*,"

"What the deuce is going on here?" Durkee asked. "You lost me, Captain."

"I have an idea that I can make some ammunition," McCracken said. "We can cast the bullets and make paper cartridges, now all we have to solve is a primer. Do you have any fulminate of mercury, Rettig?"

"*Nein, nein.*" Rettig waved his hands. "Such a thing iss too dangerous. Pooofff and der vagon iss gone. Me also."

McCracken's let down was sudden and hard. He bit his lip for a moment, then snapped his fingers. "Rettig, I'll send some men around to set up that lathe and by morning I want a mold made to cast bullets. Durkee, scout through the wagons and get every scrap of light paper you can find."

"Now?"

"Right now. Bring everything to my office. And let's keep this among ourselves." McCracken wheeled and trotted away, toward the wall near the main gate. Lieutenant Wilson Chaffee had guard duty and he came down when McCracken called to him. He followed the captain into the office and waited while McCracken lighted the lamp.

"Perhaps," McCracken said, "there is a way to temporarily ease our ammunition shortage. I found a gunsmith among the settlers."

"Gunsmith, sir? Does he have military ammunition?"

"Not a round," McCracken said. "But he has a lathe."

"You've lost me, sir," Chaffee admitted.

"Wilson, with a lathe, he can make a cherry from which to cut a forty-five caliber bullet mold. And with that we can cast bullets."

"Where will we get the lead, sir?"

"Not lead," McCracken said, "but something that will do. Pewter! We'll gather every pewter pot and candlestick in the wagon train and melt them down." He enumerated the items on his fingers. "Karopsik can get a detail together and help Rettig, the gunsmith, to set up the lathe. Have O'Fallon and a detail roust out every piece of pewter in the train. Durkee is gathering paper."

311

"Paper?"

"To make the paper cartridges," McCracken said. "Rettig has the saltpeter to soak the paper with so it will burn clean and not leave a spark in the breech to blow up the new charge in a man's face." He sat down on the desk corner. "We'll take the powder from an artillery powder bag and one round of artillery ammunition we'll never miss. The fulminate of mercury had me going for a moment, but we can use the igniting charge in the caps from one of our own artillery projectiles. The stuff's hard now but it can be scraped away and remade into a paste that'll dry. Don't you see, we can push a forty-five ball into the open breech, lay a cigarette of powder behind it, lay in a small lump of fulminate where the primer will hit it and bang away!"

"I believe it'll work," Chaffee said, and stormed out. McCracken sat for a time, considering the importance of this project. He didn't expect that this ammunition would ever come up to government issue standards, and it certainly would be more clumsy to handle. But it would shoot, and if a few pewter slugs sailed Gall's way, he might be persuaded to stay out there until Glendennon could get back from Fetterman.

Leaving the office, he walked across the parade to his own quarters.

Ness appeared to be asleep; the lamp was turned low and her uninjured arm was flung across her face. McCracken took the extra blanket from the foot of the bed and spread it over her. Then he went to his chest of drawers for a change of clothes. He made no noise and was startled when Ness said, "You're making me ashamed for taking your bed."

"That's nonsense," he said. "Go back to sleep."

"I wasn't sleeping," she said. "I was thinking. Trying to understand myself."

He could not see her distinctly; the half darkness was between them and their voices passed through it quietly.

"I've been dishonest," she said, "and I didn't want to be. It's bothered me." She paused and for a time McCracken thought that she was not going to say any more, but at last she spoke again. "My father was disturbed because I came to you with my hurt instead of to him. I guess you wondered, too."

"Your reasons must have been good," he said. "It really doesn't matter, Ness."

"Yes, it does. I'm twenty-three; Pa says I should be married. I've been asked, and I've said yes, but I've never been to a preacher. Pa wants me to be married pretty bad and has always blamed me when the man balked."

"You don't have to tell me this," McCracken said.

"I've brought you into this," she said, "and I'm sorry. You're a nice man and I had no right. I came to you because for once I wanted to meet a man on my own, someone Pa hadn't arranged for me to meet. But that wasn't the only reason, Bob. I wanted to make a man like me before he saw Pa. Like me so much that he wouldn't back away once Pa started talking his leg off. That's the way it's always been. Men shy away from me because they don't want Pa for a father-in-law."

McCracken walked over and stood by the bed. Ness Barlow looked up at him and McCracken turned up the wick on the lamp, shedding a stronger golden light on her face. "Ness," he said with suppressed amusement, "you're a man hunter."

"Yes," she said. "And I'm not ashamed."

"And on top of that, you're a conniving woman."

"All women are conniving," she said. "Some hide it, that's all."

McCracken bent over her. "I haven't said so yet, but you're an honest woman, and they're damned rare." He watched her carefully, marveling that he had not noticed before how attractive she was. "I've treated you rough, got you drunk, and compromised you in your father's eyes. Are you honest enough to know when a man wants to go the next step?"

She answered him by reaching up to grab his neckerchief and pull him toward her. He held himself back so as not to hurt her arm but there was nothing gentle in his kiss, or her answer.

He raised up slowly and said, "You did what you wanted to do, Ness. I wouldn't care if your father talked in his confounded sleep."

She looked at him a moment longer, then quickly turned her face away. "Please," she said. "Just let me be with this for a while."

He left her and walked back to Chaffee's quarters to lie on the hard pallet with his hands propped behind his head, thinking about the step he had just taken, a step he had avoided for quite a few years. When he had walked into her room a short time ago he had thought of Ness Barlow as simply a nice girl who needed a little help over the rough spots. But now he pictured her in a kitchen fixing his supper, and afterward, while he was playing with his fine sons, talking to him while she sewed, giving a new purpose and dimension to his life.

That he could even consider these things now was a little crazy, but the thought stayed with him and he carried it from wakefulness into sleep and the dreams became more vivid than his waking thoughts.

★ ★ ★

First Lieutenant Harry Glendennon had left his hunting-case watch behind, but as he decided it must be near one o'clock, the Sioux jumped him. He had no warning that they were anywhere near; a bowstring thrummed and a shaft of flame entered his right side, passed through, and left him in a state of shock. By sheer habit his hand flipped toward his holster, and by some miracle of inner will he fired the revolver, watching a brave tumble from a horse that seemed to appear from nowhere.

Shots were fired. His horse screamed and went down thrashing, and other lances of flame seared through Harry Glendennon's body. One high up in the lung. Another that shattered his left arm. Glendennon was on his knees and shooting while blood welled up in his mouth, strangling him until he let it pour forth unchecked.

The night was a-sparkle with gun muzzles flashing, and he spun around twice as he was hit again. Another Indian sagged from his pony and fell heavily on his carbine. The gun in Glendennon's hand recoiled against his palm, but it grew intolerably heavy until finally he had to put it down and rest. Slowly, like a wax figure melting, he sagged forward and lay still.

Gall was the first to dismount. He flung off his pony and turned Glendennon over on his back, bending close to study the man's relaxed features in the night light. There was a run of guttural talk and one of the Sioux gathered up the reins of a pony while others lifted Glendennon and tied him well.

The Indians Glendennon downed were down for good; Gall looked at them briefly and then they were borne away, back to the Sioux camp near Fort Runyon. But Gall and three others remained. All carried rifles as well as the bows they used so efficiently.

This night fighting was not to their liking, and because of it, they believed that two of their brothers would wander in darkness for eternity. But Chief Gall had spoken: the road to Fetterman must be closed. If nothing else was blocked, it did not matter. But supplies came from Fetterman.

Mounted again, Gall led his party slowly down the pass toward Fort Runyon. Several hours later they reached the flats. Gall's raised hand halted them. He took the braided grass rein of the pony bearing Glendennon and went on alone.

★ ★ ★

Private George Gilcrest had the honor of sighting Chief Gall as he approached the wall; and he fired the first shot, missing the chief by a dozen feet. Had Gilcrest spent more time at the rifle butts he might, with that one shot, have ended an Indian campaign; but he missed, and Gall did not give him a second chance. With a long, blood-freezing wail, Gall stormed away, leaving the pony with its grisly burden behind.

Gall's shout was enough to wake every man on the post; it brought Captain Robert McCracken bolt upright. He stormed out of the quarters like a man starting a long race and making certain he had a fast start.

A group was gathering around Private Gilcrest, who gestured wildly and shouted nothing that made sense.

Lieutenant O'Fallon, however, made sense of it all. As soon as he spotted the laden horse, he ordered a detail out to retrieve him.

McCracken was standing by the gate when the detail came back. Someone came up with a lantern and one look was enough. Gall, wanting to make certain that the army understood that Glendennon had not fought a chicken fight, had thrust his empty revolver into his belt. The six bullets holes and the arrow sticking out of Harry Glendennon told the rest of the story: this was one soldier who had gone down trying.

"Lift him off easy," McCracken said. The movers' camp, too, was wide awake, and it would only be moments now before the curious gathered. "O'Fallon, head those farmers off. Get them back to their wagons. This is our business."

"Yes, sir."

"Into headquarters with him," McCracken said. "Karopsik, see that a grave is dug for morning burial." He turned then and walked to Glendennon's quarters. McCracken knocked four times and, not getting an answer, he went in uninvited. When he lighted the lamp and flashed it in the bedroom, he could understand why Sheila had not answered the door. An empty whisky bottle stood on the chest of drawers. She lay across the bed, snoring.

For a moment McCracken's disgust almost overwhelmed him, but he turned away and went back outside to stand on the porch. After a while he could think of Sheila Glendennon with pity. In a way she was somewhat like a prostitute who kept a pimp in order that she might look at him and know that she was not as low as one could go.

Shaking his head, McCracken went back across the parade, bumping into Mike Janis who was coming through the wagon park. "I heard," Janis said. "How's the ammunition coming? It had better be really good now."

"Let's find out," McCracken said,

and together they walked to Rettig's wagon. He had the cherry made and was cutting the mold. To save time, several troopers were melting pewter in a cast-iron kettle. Three more rolled cigarette cartridges, while two others, under Chaffee's guidance, handled the dangerous job of forming fulminate of mercury into pea-sized pellets.

"We'll be able to test it in the morning," McCracken said.

"I won't be here to see it," Janis said evenly.

"What the hell is that supposed to mean?"

"I'm leavin'," Janis said. "Glendennon failed, didn't he? Well, I won't. I'm more Injun than Gall, and you sure ain't goin' to do much fightin' with them home-rolled cigarettes."

"True, but you're not going any place," McCracken said.

"Bob, don't be a damn fool now. I can make it, and besides, if I don't, who's to cry? Marta's got her man now and I'm happy about it. There's no more use in me hangin' around. They'll be raisin' kids one of these days, and I wouldn't want to give 'em any of my Injun ways." He paused to spit and hitch up his pants. "Naw, I don't want to hear a lot of argument, Bob. I'm goin' and that's that. And I ain't comin' back. I'll tell the colonel what's happened, then light out. Lots of room in Texas — I hear tell they're havin' Comanche trouble down there."

"What can I say, Mike?"

"Be best to keep your danged mouth shut," Janis said. "You can see that I get a good horse, though."

McCracken could think of many arguments, but none of them strong enough. The homemade ammunition wouldn't make a dent in an all-out fight; they had to get more from Fetterman. And who knew how to shinny through a Sioux blockade better than Janis?

"All right," McCracken agreed. "I'll have one waiting at the gate when you're ready." He offered his hand but

Janis just snorted and turned away.

"You know I don't hold with that nonsense." He walked off, his body rolling with the peculiar gait that had taken him across vast wilderness and through countless dangers.

McCracken found the cavalry sergeant and had him select a horse. Somehow, he could not bring himself to watch Janis leave, so he went back to his own quarters and found Ness awake. She was out of bed and brewing a pot of coffee. Lacking a robe, she had a blanket wound around her, trailing one end on the floor as she walked.

"Was there trouble?"

"Yes," he said. "I sent a man out. The Indians brought him back dead."

She did not say how terrible this was or any of the other hollow things and he was grateful for her silence. Ness did not know Glendennon and she did not pretend to a grief she could not feel. But she looked at McCracken and understood how he felt. She offered him a cup of coffee.

"Was he someone special, Bob?"

"Special? Yes, in a way I guess he was. Maybe not a very good way, but he was changing. I was pretty sure of that when he volunteered to ride alone to Fetterman. I'm dead sure of it now."

She moved to the window, and stood looking out. "It's getting light," she said quietly.

"Then I think a long day is beginning for me," he said.

When he stepped out on the porch he noticed that the settlers were getting out of their wagons and breakfast fires springing up on the parade. The guard relief was changing; Borgnine moved a fresh detail to the palisade wall and set them to their posts.

At first the familiar routine had a steadying effect on McCracken. His thoughts turned to Gall, and he wondered how he was faring. Probably he was squatting before a fire, eating jerked venison while his squaw sewed patiently on a pair of new moccasins.

But routine became a dull monotony that grew heavier as each hour passed. Night came again after an interminable wait. Night and day, with agonizing regularity, until a chain of them became a week. McCracken had to keep his command busy. He had repairs made on several buildings, and this helped pass the time. One hand on the rifle, the other on a hammer . . . one eye on the job, the other peering over the wall.

Apparently the Sioux were taking a rest, too.

Then the Sioux grew tired of resting. McCracken was starting for the ramp ladder when one of the guards shouted and the air was filled with ringing whoops and the ground began to reverberate with the pound of horses' hoofs. McCracken broke into a run. Borgnine was shouting to the battery in place at the end of the wall. The men began hauling on their gun tackle, swinging the heavy piece around toward the charging Sioux.

Once on the wall, McCracken stood

motionless, held there by the savage pageantry before him. They charged in a line abreast, nearly a hundred mounted warriors, all Gall could muster now. The range closed with alarming speed. Borgnine gave the command to fire without prompting, and both pieces mounted on the end platforms belched and recoiled against the restraining tackle. Against such a target the gunners could only lay down their fire ahead of the rushing line, hoping that they judged close enough so that the Sioux would run into it; and perhaps they succeeded, for slight gaps appeared when the dirt and smoke cleared. But the Sioux came on without slacking their pace, leaving only a scatter of downed and dying behind.

The interval between the hostiles and the wall was now five hundred yards and closing fast. Again the artillery sounded, and one of the rounds passed over the Sioux, bursting behind them with no other effect than to shower dirt. McCracken felt suddenly chilled, and knew with numbing clarity that this time his wonderful weapons would not stop Chief Gall. He turned and shouted, "Every man on the wall! Riflemen! Use the homemade stuff. Save the issue rounds until last. They load faster."

Borgnine was firing as rapidly as possible, but Gall was making a final bid; he refused to be stopped this time. McCracken did not look at the Sioux; he already knew the results.

What remained of Harry Glendennon's cavalry troop was coming onto the palisade wall, carbines ready. Major Davis drew his men into formation and led them across the parade at a run. Apparently Davis wasn't as anxious to be a dead hero — or traitor — as he'd indicated earlier.

Lieutenant Borgnine raced up. "Three hundred and fifty yards, Captain! My God, we can't stop them!"

When McCracken looked, Gall had shaved the distance fifty yards more. The artillery fire had not been without effect; but Gall had kept pulling his rent line together and still presented a solid, formidable front.

"Give the command to fire in volley at two hundred yards," McCracken said, his voice surprisingly calm. Borgnine gave him an odd look but said nothing. He wheeled away, bellowing the order.

Men settled down behind their carbines and waited; then at Borgnine's hand signal, they roared in unison, and while they crammed paper shells into the guns, another section belched a volley. Davis and his command took a position, but their fire was disorganized, too rapid; McCracken knew that he could not stop them now, but Davis was throwing ammunition away. Ammunition they could not spare.

The carbine fire was having some effect; a few of Gall's braves toppled and fell away, but the main body was not stopped. Bullets slammed into the wall. One man fell back, hand clamped over his breast. A few arrows whirred overhead to land helter-skelter among the wagons below. A woman screamed. A child began to cry. Borgnine's section was taking the load of the fight with their disciplined fire, while Davis's men banged away.

The wall was becoming a hot place, bullets whined and snapped and another man sighed before tumbling to the ground below. Gall and his warriors were so close now that the soldiers had to lean over the palisade edge to fire down at them. The rain of arrows stopped and instead came a shower of ropes, thin and strong, each with a crude hook or a stout stick on the end, anything that might catch and hold long enough for a man to scale.

The guns were used mainly as clubs now as the lip of the wall became a froth of surging bodies, some blue-clad, some naked. Even Davis fought like a madman, clubbing with his carbine.

McCracken was pulping a face with the butt of his revolver, screaming his accumulated hate. The sound was a blend of cries and curses, of shots and the hollowness of bones breaking under smashing blows, and men's last words before death closed them off. Each man who teetered on the wall, Sioux and soldier alike, moved without thought, with instincts given direction only by the urge to kill before they were killed.

McCracken lost all sense of time, knowing in his fury only the bitter taste of fear, and in the end a deep gratitude and surprise that he was still alive.

Chief Gall led his men with fanatical courage, but he did not break over the wall. A few did and were slain, along with the soldiers who tried to stop them; but in the end, Gall was forced to fall back, to suffer his losses and retreat out of range. And with his retreat the sound died away.

McCracken forced himself to gather the remnant of his command into some semblance of order. An immediate count of the dead was taken. Thirteen men; he could not have spared five.

The wounded would have to look after themselves for the time being.

About McCracken men sat and looked vacantly around without focus or direction. One man kept snapping his empty carbine until Lieutenant Chaffee took it away from him. Chaffee was limping from a bullet-pierced thigh, but when Sergeant Karopsik offered to tend it, Chaffee pushed him away with a curse.

Five Sioux lay on the parade where they had toppled from the wall. The settlers gathered around them, their faces animal-curious as though they could not make up their minds whether to ignore them or kick them. McCracken caught Borgnine's eye and motioned him over. There was a grayness to the officer's heavy face.

"Try to straighten this up," McCracken said. "Details to care for the wounded. Take them to the wagons. See that the women do what they can for them."

"Yes, sir," Borgnine said. "Sir, I didn't think we were going to make it."

"Neither did I," McCracken told him. "Have O'Fallon get an ammunition count, but do it quietly. Have Rettig make some more. That shot pretty good."

"Yes, sir, it sure as hell did."

McCracken turned away and started down the ladder, pausing when he saw Elwood Davis groping about, picking up the empty brass cartridges. "Souvenier hunting, Mr. Davis?"

The man looked around guiltily. "They can be reloaded," Davis said, his voice dull. "I know they can be reloaded." He was almost like a child who had done irreparable damage and was now doing his best to atone for it.

Big Jim Durkee was trying to bring some order to the settlers. Marta gathered the women quickly and with their help made ready to receive the wounded that Borgnine was lowering off the wall.

McCracken turned to Borgnine. "We can't talk here. Let's go to my office."

He followed him and once inside,

Borgnine closed the door. He leaned against it and said, "That was mighty close, Captain. Can we take another one like that?"

"No," McCracken said honestly. "Not unless we can make a lot more ammunition."

Durkee came in then, his expression angry. "By God, they told us the army'd look after us!" He wiped the back of his hand across his mouth. "There are the women and children to think of, Captain."

"You don't have to remind me," McCracken said. "I'll be honest with you, Durkee. We're nearly out of ammunition. But maybe we can make some more in time."

The man's shoulders sagged. "We'll likely die here? You trying to say that, Captain?"

"We're not dead yet. Durkee, keep this to yourself. I don't want a panic started among the women."

He went out with Borgnine and they walked to Alex Rettig's wagon. More of the paper-wrapped ammunition was laid out neatly in a wooden box. Rettig came from the wagon, polishing his glasses on a blue handkerchief.

"Iss some done," he said. "That it vill vork iss sure, but how goot it shoots iss any man's guess."

"As good as the other, I hope," McCracken said. Borgnine commandeered a carbine from a private passing by. He brought it back to McCracken, who took one of the paper cartridges and opened the breech. The cartridge went in well, until the pewter bullet shoved against the barrel lands and when McCracken closed the breech, the paper broke.

Rettig was saying, "Der danger, *Hauptmann*, iss dat dere iss no case to hold der explosion. Powder may blow back through der firing pin hole. Maybe put out der eyes."

"Hold it away from you when you fire it, Captain," Borgnine suggested. "Just because the first lot worked doesn't mean this new batch will."

McCracken walked clear of the wagons and faced the south wall, a distance of sixty yards. An old half-rotten canteen hung there as a target and McCracken cocked the carbine. Shouldering it quickly, he sighted and squeezed off. The pewter bullet had a healthy charge of powder behind it and the recoil belted him back, but the canteen flipped up and spun to the ground.

Rettig had been right. Black powder smoke curled lazily from the carbine's mechanism, escaping back through the firing pin hole in the hinged breech block, but there was no damage. The breech opened smoothly and McCracken blew out the bore.

"Mr. Borgnine, see that Sergeant Karopsik gets some more of these cartridges right away. And if you can find Chaffee, and if his leg doesn't bother him too much, have him make another two hundred." He handed the carbine to Alex Rettig and walked away. Crossing the parade, he stopped a moment to observe the care the wounded were getting from the settlers' wives. Marta was there, and when she saw him, she came up.

"You had no right to send Pop. No right at all."

"I couldn't have stopped him," McCracken said. "Marta, he was right. I couldn't have spared an officer. Mike understood the hole I was in and he tried to pull me out of it. I'm grateful to him."

She looked at him as though she suspected a lie, but at last she saw that this was the truth. "I guess I knew," she said dully. "You get a feeling about things like that."

Ever since her return from Fetterman, Marta had forsaken her men's clothes for a dress. She had taken some other unnoticed step that made her more womanly, and perhaps Mike Janis had seen this before he left. Perhaps this was the reason he had gone, because he felt there was no more reason for him in her life.

She said, "He ain't coming back, is he?"

"Girl, he'll make it. Mike's smarter than that!"

She shook her head. "Oh, I guess he'll get through all right. I mean he's not coming back to me, is he?" She searched McCracken's expression and found her answer there. "That's the way he'd do it, just up and leave me, now that Fields — " Suddenly there were tears in her voice. "He's my pop. How can I tell him that he never has to leave me?"

"He'll know," McCracken said. "Marta, he'll realize he was wrong. One of these days he'll come riding up and you'll hand him a grandson to dance on his knee."

"I want to believe that, Bob. But it's hard, knowing Pop." She tried a smile and achieved a fair one. Then she went back to her work and McCracken continued his circle of the parade. He met Lieutenant O'Fallon near the stable yard.

"Sir," O'Fallon said, saluting, "I have a detail digging graves."

"All right," McCracken said absently. "The heat is getting bad." He walked on to headquarters and stood on the porch, breathing heavily. There was a fine film of sweat on his face and he wiped it with his neckerchief before going back across the parade.

5

ANOTHER week dragged by, a week of molten sun that dried and darkened the skin of every man on the post and parched the parade into a mass of irregular cracks. McCracken was kept busy with the staggering job of complete reorganization, the fortifying of his command with his seriously depleted forces.

Chief Gall's fanatical attack had left no doubt in McCracken's mind that Fort Runyon was under an active state of seige. His blockhouses, designed for guarding the pass, were now worthless and he had the two artillery pieces removed and brought back to the confines of the post.

Traditionally, the Sioux preferred high ground from which to launch their attack, and he knew they would not break a long standing habit now. The pass was too far away to assault Runyon, and the land in two other directions was too flat. All that remained was the hill, and it was there that they moved their camp. If another attack came, and he was sure it would, all military might would have to be concentrated on the hill.

Once the artillery had been moved and repositioned, McCracken called a meeting of his officers. Chaffee was absent, his wound had lamed him so that he could hardly walk, but he still remained on duty.

O'Fallon showed the most amount of wear. He was a seasoned man now; the gaiety had fled from his eyes, leaving him a serious-minded soldier. Borgnine, who was older, had long ago learned to take the bad with the good; and aside from his obvious weariness he seemed unchanged.

"Gentlemen," McCracken said, "until now I've been unable to fire on the hostiles at any but point-blank range.

And I think Gall believes that our artillery won't shoot any farther."

"How do you figure that, sir?" O'Fallon asked.

"Because he's perched in his camp on the other side of that hill," McCracken said flatly. "Any commander who knew artillery range would be at least two and a half miles from here. Gall, I'm sure, thinks he's out of reach. I've been hoping to lure him in closer, and it's my intention to teach him a lesson." McCracken went to the open door and pointed. "I want the trails of the pieces buried so deep that the muzzles are elevated nearly sixty degrees; those are my calculations and they are accurate enough. We can make minor corrections in elevation to a plus or minus ten degrees while the guns are in that position."

"Mortars?" Borgnine asked.

McCracken faced him. "Yes, Gus. We're going to lay in a barrage on the other side of that hill that will

343

make Gall think he's got a front row seat in hell."

"We need an observation post," O'Fallon said.

"And we have one," McCracken said. "The flagpole. By my estimate, it's sixty or seventy feet high, a devilish length for a flag, but a good lodge pine and big enough for a man to climb. I think Sergeant Heinzman will be the logical choice. With a pair of binoculars he should be able to observe the bursts."

"By God!" Borgnine said. "I'll get those pits dug in no time." He stormed out, shouting as he ran across the parade.

"You have work to do, Mr. O'Fallon," McCracken said.

"Yes, sir!"

The civilians grumbled a little when Borgnine forced them to move their wagons, huddling them even closer together. McCracken observed the digging and the placing of the artillery for a time, then walked to his quarters and found Ness Barlow getting ready to move out. She had been up and around for some time, but McCracken had persuaded her to stay on.

"I'm ashamed that I've stayed so long as it is," she told him now.

"You've been most welcome," McCracken said. "Your presence has brightened this dreary place."

He left then to go to the stable yard where a small detachment of cavalry was billeted. Davis was there and quite sober. He looked at McCracken and said, "I've — ah — taken over for Mr. Glendennon."

"Oh?" McCracken murmured. "Carry on, then." He no longer blamed Davis for anything; the time for blame was past. Walking slowly he made his way to headquarters and found Ness Barlow standing there. She was watching a detail prepare for burial three of the wounded who had at last given up the fight. When the task was finished, Lieutenant Chaffee read a short passage from the Bible. The men picked up their shovels again.

McCracken found the sound of dirt sliding off the spades intolerable. He took Ness Barlow's arm and walked away with her. She remained silent because his manner indicated that he preferred it; he found it remarkable that she should sense his moods so quickly.

Finally he said, "Ness, if you could leave here tomorrow, where would you go?"

"I really hadn't thought about it," she said. "I was leaving it up to you. Perhaps I'm taking a lot for granted because we haven't talked too much about it."

Her words surprised him, yet they seemed quite natural and he realized then that he had been preparing for them subconsciously. "I'm army," McCracken said. "That's different from farming. Nothing settled. Moving whenever some general decides I should."

"I'm moving now," she said. "Bob, I'm not afraid of new things."

"No, I guess you're not." He paused.

"I'll have to tell your father, Ness."

"I'll tell him," she said. "He wouldn't believe you." She smiled. "He won't believe me either, but I'll tell him just the same."

"Why do I love you, Ness? How? In such a short time? Can you understand it when it seems we have no time left to love?"

"Whether we have time or not isn't important," she said. Her hand touched his arm, then she bent forward and quickly kissed him. "I must go now. My place is with the movers; I'm needed there."

He watched her go toward the wagons, then walked over to the new gun positions. There was some doubt in his mind about the trails being buried like that; the recoil might drive them hopelessly into the ground; but then he saw that Borgnine had already considered that possibility and placed timbers behind them to absorb the shock.

A few minutes later Borgnine joined

him, his shirt sweat-soaked. "All ready, sir."

"Get Heinzman up the flagpole," McCracken said.

The sergeant was already rigging a bo'sun's chair and a snubbing rope to hold him in place once he'd climbed to the top. He was given a boost and up he went, pausing several times to catch his breath. Finally he made himself fast and unsheathed his field glasses. His observation was brief, but complete. He called down, "Captain, I can see the tops of their lodges about fifty or seventy-five yards on the other side of the rise."

"Thank you, Sergeant. Observe our fire." McCracken turned to Gustave Borgnine. "Fire when ready, two pieces at a time."

"Aye, sir."

The others had heard and breeches were slammed shut on full powder bags. Borgnine signaled; and the two end guns roared, slamming back, spitting thick, acrid smoke over the parade.

For a moment Heinzman was obscured by the cloud, then twin booms echoed from the other side of the hill and Heinzman shouted, "Short! Twenty yards!"

"Up three degrees!" Borgnine barked and the adjustment was made.

"Fire for effect," McCracken said, clapping his hands over his ears to kill the concussion. The settlers stood in a pressed group, observing this with a bit of awe.

"On target!" Heinzman shouted. "On target, Captain!"

"Fire in relays," McCracken said.

"In relays!" Borgnine shouted.

From that moment on, the air was solid sound and the artillery men sweated over their guns, feeding shot and powder as soon as the bore could be blown clear and the ammunition passed. McCracken kept his eye on the rounds expended, for his supply was limited.

From the top of the flagpole, Heinzman was screaming something and McCracken strained to make it out. Smoke was a dense haze, held by the walls and the still air.

"Cease firing!" McCracken shouted and the din died away, leaving a great hole of silence.

Heinzman's yelling was clear now, but McCracken did not need the sergeant's report; he could hear the ringing lilt of a bugle and for a time could not believe that this was not a trick of his hearing. A soldier on the wall pointed excitedly.

"Captain, it's the damned colonel!"

McCracken ran to an up-ladder and made his own observation. Streaming from the pass were two companies of United States Cavalry, and in the lead was Brubaker; McCracken recognized the regimental colors. They came on in a column of fours, at a gallop. McCracken almost laughed at the irony of it, for again Brubaker was conducting a token maneuver. Still, there would be no humor when Brubaker arrived; this would be salt on an old wound.

There was a cloud of smoke billowing up with tongues of flame half hidden by the hill. The exploding shells had ignited the tinder-dry lodges. Even at this distance McCracken could hear the yelling of the disorganized Sioux.

Brubaker held on his pace and had reached the first blockhouse. On the flagpole, Heinzman was studying the whole thing through his field glasses and trying to shout down his report, but his voice was lost as the settlers crowded along the wall, all talking at once, some cheering, others crying without shame.

The Sioux rout was completely hidden from those on the ground at Fort Runyon, but everyone could hear the sounds of their terror. Finally a party of mounted Sioux raced away to the north. McCracken had anticipated a revengeful attack; but when the Sioux disappeared from sight and did not come back, he knew that Gall was finally whipped.

The sense of relief swept through

351

the post as a thrill; everyone laughed and shouted like children. McCracken turned to Lieutenant Borgnine and said, "Let's get some semblance of order here, Gus. The colonel will be in shortly and we don't want him to think we run an untidy post." The last contained a note of sarcasm which Borgnine did not miss.

"No," Borgnine said, smiling, "we wouldn't want that." He turned to go, then stopped, pointing toward the pass. McCracken followed his arm and saw a wagon and a detail of ten men tipping down. They came on at a more sedate pace, as though they carried a precious cargo.

"Get ready to let them in," McCracken said and went down the ladder.

His first task was to relieve the crowded condition of Runyon's parade ground, and this was done by ordering the movers to establish a camp outside the palisade walls near the main gate. The men hitched up hurriedly, the women packing the gear they had used for camping. At long last the parade was clear and McCracken saw that Brubaker was holding his command outside the walls until the settlers had finished filing through the gate.

The wagon and its tender cargo was less than a mile away now, coming on slowly. McCracken stood by the gate to watch as the detail finally made the post and filed in. The young lieutenant in charge gave very crisp commands that dismounted his men. Stripping off his gloves, he came up and saluted, then offered his hand.

"I'm late, I see," he said. "May I introduce myself? I'm Lieutenant Finlay Chalmers, 5th Infantry."

"Where is your company?" McCracken asked.

"You see it there," Chalmers said, a bit smugly. He was an apple-cheeked young man, brash and bubbling with confidence.

"The colonel's coming," one of the guards yelled.

"Excuse me," McCracken said.

"Of course," Chalmers said. "May I look at your artillery? A limited weapon, but interesting."

Had not Colonel Truman Brubaker been coming through the main gate, McCracken would have taken the time to dress down this upstart officer to bite-size, but he swallowed the urge and turned away.

The colonel dismounted from his horse while the remainder of his command trooped onto the post toward the stable yard. Brubaker's florid face was even more colorful than usual and he puffed as he moved his bulk about, stamping feeling back into his legs.

"Just what were you firing at over the brow of that hill?" Brubaker asked.

"Gall finally moved his camp within range, Colonel. He was drumming up his courage to make another try to take the fort."

"Take it?" Brubaker looked around. He could count and not many remained in McCracken's command to count. "I must say when you reported your losses I could hardly believe it. However, I see that your figures were modest."

"More than half," McCracken said quietly. "We've been under severe attack here, sir."

"I can see that," Brubaker said impatiently "But it hardly justifies such a loss of men. This won't look at all well on your record, Robert." He looked around the post. "Where is Brevet Major Davis, Captain?"

"I'll have him summoned," McCracken turned to a near-by soldier. "Get Davis here on the double, Collins."

"Yes, sir." He trotted away and McCracken gave the colonel his full attention.

"I don't see Mr. Dandridge with you, Colonel."

Brubaker was lighting a cigar; he spoke around it. "Mr. Dandridge chose to remain at Fetterman. Something or other to do with his paper." His glance raised quickly to McCracken. "It was unfortunate that a correspondent had to be present and record this dismal campaign. Had it been only a matter of military record, perhaps I could have salvaged something for you, Bob." He spread his hands in a futile gesture. "But if it has been made public . . . "

"I quite understand," McCracken said. He fell silent as Elwood Davis rushed up, his hands making minor adjustments to his uniform.

"Ah, there, Davis," Brubaker said. "I want to see you." His glance moved past Davis to two of McCracken's soldier's. "Come here, you two." They looked at each other, each wondering what past sin had finally caught up with them. "Place Major Davis under close arrest," Brubaker said. "He is to talk with no one without my written permission."

The soldiers bracketed Davis, who stood dumbly. "Sir!"

"Major, I'm not an idiot. I discovered, through a routine inventory, the discrepancy in the ammunition ration. Of course I realized what you had done." He waved his hand. "Take him and lock him up." Then he took a deep breath and found some soothing effect in his cigar. When Davis was out of earshot, Brubaker glanced again at McCracken, who was studying the colonel carefully.

"Sir, when did you make the discovery?"

Brubaker frowned, then said, "Nearly eight days ago."

"I see. Did you expect us to be dead when you arrived?"

"Frankly, I did," Brubaker said. "But then, you have always been a disappointment to me, Bob. I would say that you have scattered Gall, not defeated him."

"This has proved very convenient for you, hasn't it, sir? I mean, Davis's bringing a short ammunition ration. It fit beautifully into your general plan to make me out a pig-head who bumbled and lost my command."

"Yes," Brubaker said. "Bob, I'm a clean man; my record will attest to that. Look at my reports and you'll find them truthful, although not optimistic. There is nothing on record by me that cannot be construed to be anything but caution. My years in service have taught me to cover my tracks." He stepped on his cigar and smiled. "I'd like a table set up in your quarters. Say an hour?"

"Very well, sir." Brubaker started to walk away, but stopped when McCracken added, "Colonel, who the hell is this Chalmers?"

"So you've met the engaging young man?" Brubaker smiled. "Fine boy. Good family. He'll go far in the service. Very far. No doubt you'll become fast friends."

McCracken doubted it. Leaving the post, he went into the wagon camp; they were making up to leave. Big Jim Durkee gave McCracken as good a reason for moving on as a farmer could have: "Gettin' late in the season, and a man's got to get the seed in if he expects it to grow." He offered

358

his hand. "You've done good by us, Captain. Likely we'll never forget you for it."

"Thank you," McCracken said. "I wish you all a lot of luck."

"I guess we'll do what you do, make our own." He turned then and finished his hitching. McCracken moved slowly through the camp, his mind still troubled by the fact that Fields Dandridge hadn't come in with the colonel's command. He wondered if Dandridge had met with an accident somewhere along the way. He would have to find out from one of the sergeants; Brubaker would never tell him the truth.

At the Barlow wagon he stopped. Barlow was standing by the off wheel, his face wearing its habitual expression of impatience. Ness was in the wagon and Barlow had been talking to her, stopping when McCracken came up.

"My girl says she's not going on," Barlow said flatly. "That's nonsense, that's what it is. Pure nonsense." He waved his hands aimlessly. "What's here beside Injuns?" He shook his head. "You two in love? I don't believe it. Knew something would happen when she went to you. Knew it in my bones. This ain't a natural life. Not like farmin'. Besides, what's goin' to happen to me? I want my girl near so I can help her."

Ness came from the wagon and lifted down a small trunk. She pulled it around to the side of the wagon and stopped by McCracken's side. "He wants me, Pa. And he loves me. No one's ever wanted me and loved me before at the same time."

Barlow said, very disgusted, "You don't know your own mind."

"I'm not going with you, Pa." She offered him her hand but he would not take it, placing his own firmly behind him.

"All right, Pa. Good-by then." She looked once at McCracken, then turned away.

"Ness!" This was a shout, and a

plea. "Girl, don't leave me alone!"

"You've got to be alone sometime, Pa." She looked steadily at him. "I'm in love, Pa. Nothing else matters. Not you, nor nobody. I'm going to be happy like I've never been before. Maybe you can come and see us sometime after you get settled."

She walked away from him and entered the post. McCracken felt sorry for this man who could not understand a simple truth, but there was nothing he could do about it.

"Good-by, Mr. Barlow," McCracken said. "And good luck."

"Agh!" Barlow whipped around and stood with his back stiff and hostile. McCracken waited a moment, then picked up Ness's small trunk and carried it to his own quarters.

A detail of enlisted men was busy erecting a long table so the Colonel Truman Brubaker could hold his dinner later. They looked questioningly at Ness, but McCracken steered her into the bedroom to unpack her things.

When he closed the door, she said, "I think curtains would be nice. And I have some cloth for the table." She smiled, but there was a tinge of sadness in it. "Perhaps there is a soldier who can make some furniture."

"Yes," McCracken said. "We have a carpenter." He set the trunk down. "I have to feed the colonel tonight, Ness. Will you be with me?"

"Yes," she said. Slowly tears started from the corners of her eyes and she turned her back to him so he could not see her cry. "I'm sorry for Pa. I wanted it to be different, but he would never let go of me. And he's got to let go." She dried her eyes. "Would you open the trunk for me? The lock sticks."

"Sure." He opened it, then went into the other room as the soldiers were leaving. When he started to close the door he paused to watch Reese Barlow walking toward the porch. He stopped, hat in his hand. He moved his feet self-consciously, then said, "I'm a danged fool, son. I didn't even say good-by proper to Nessie."

"Come on in," McCracken said, a deep pleasure in his voice. Ness had heard and came to the bedroom door. She waited; her father had to begin. There was no other way and Reese Barlow understood that.

He said, "Forgive me, Nessie. Losin' your ma was more than I could rightly stand. And I made you take her place, Nessie. That was wrong, wasn't it?"

"You couldn't help it, Pa. No one ever really blamed you."

He nodded. "It eases me to hear you say that, Nessie. When I get settled, I want you to come and visit with me, both of you. Will you do that?"

She came to him quickly and put her arms around him. "We'll come, Pa. That's a promise."

Barlow had to leave, or wanted to. He pushed her away gently and offered McCracken his hand. "Trouble was, you're more man than I ever had to deal with before. That scared me.

Made me say and do things I'm rightly sorry for."

"Don't be," McCracken said gently.

"Well," Barlow said. "Time to be goin'. I ain't sad, Nessie. Not a sick inside kind of sad."

"I know, Pa. I know."

He gave them each a brief smile, then walked away. McCracken closed the door and Ness said, "That's the way I wanted it to be, Bob. Everything that's good has come to me now."

"I think the good's only beginning," he said.

★ ★ ★

Captain McCracken dreaded the officers' dinner; yet he knew that he would be there, a target for Colonel Truman Brubaker's barbed observations. Feeding these men in a room scarcely twelve feet square took some doing, but Ness Barlow was up to it. Unable to work efficiently with her splinted arm, she bossed four of McCracken's soldiers and made them like it. When darkness came, she had the lamps lighted and a cloth placed on the table. McCracken was taking a final tour of the post, worrying about Fields Dandridge, and what he would say to Marta; she would feel that Dandridge failed to return because of her.

He knew this was not true, but his knowledge would be of no importance to Marta; he felt a genuine helplessness. In passing Glendennon's quarters, he stopped for a moment, and while he stood there; the door opened and Sheila came out. His first impulse was to walk away and leave her standing there, but he did not.

She said, "Where do I go now, Bob?"

He shrugged. "You'll find some place,"

"There's no place."

He shook his head. "There's always some place, Sheila."

He walked on then and she called to him but he did not stop. On his own porch he paused and listened to the pleasant sounds coming from within; the officers had gathered. Through the window, he observed Ness moving about. She offered the colonel a light for his cigar and McCracken smiled; she was a better diplomat than he suspected. She wore a white dress, completely unadorned, but she seemed like a queen with her composure. Her flaxen hair was simply braided, divided by a center part. Suddenly it seemed to McCracken that he was no longer at Fort Runyon, squatting amid miles of nothing, but in a ballroom where royalty waited and the troubles he had known never had existed.

A flurry of sound drew his attention toward the main gate, and when two soldiers shouldered it open, McCracken walked over. The first man he saw was Fields Dandridge, but Dandridge was not alone. In the glare of lantern light, Dandridge dismounted, then saw he McCracken.

"Captain, I would like to introduce

General Chase." He stepped aside and a tall, gaunt man with heavy mutton-chop whiskers moved into the breech. McCracken drew into a heel-cracking salute, then took the hand General Lucius Chase offered.

"Mr. Dandridge was good enough to wait at Fetterman for my ambulance," Chase said. His voice was a rumble, like thunderclaps echoing from a cloud bank of silence. He looked around the post and read correctly the signs of battle. "Captain, your name has appeared on my desk with startling regularity lately."

"Is that so, sir?" McCracken felt that he had to say something.

"Yes," Chase said slowly. "Colonel Brubaker has sent me quite a few reports, and I have also been reading about you in Mr. Dandridge's paper. There seems to be some conflict of view there."

"I'm sure that can be cleared up," Dandridge said. "My accounts are eye-witness, sir."

"That remains to be seen," Chase murmured. He glanced toward McCracken's quarters where light cascaded from every window. "A celebration, Captain?"

"Ah, the colonel, sir. A party in celebration of his arrival."

"A damned foolish notion," Chase said, then paused to beat the dust from his clothes. "Well, let's go, shall we?"

McCracken glanced at Dandridge, who shrugged, then they followed the general across the parade. Allowing him to get three or four paces ahead gave Dandridge the opportunity to explain. "He came out of the blue, Captain. My paper wired me that he was on his way, without escort, and would I meet him? Your guess is as good as mine about what he's up to."

Fortunately there was an orderly at McCracken's door and he sent his shout, "Attention!" like a thrown bomb into the room ahead of the general. Brubaker nearly upset his soup rising quickly and General Lucius Chase stopped amid a forest of immobile officers.

"At ease, gentlemen," he said. "Perhaps you can find a place there for me. Ah, thank you, Lieutenant." He sat down and several more chairs were placed around the table for McCracken and Dandridge.

But Dandridge did not want to stay and McCracken understood why.

As soon as he went out, a complete silence fell over the assembly. General Chase raised his head and looked around him, letting his glance settle on Truman Brubaker. "Good to see you again, Colonel. It's been a few years, hasn't it?"

"Yes, sir," Brubaker said. He put his soup spoon down and waited.

"Don't let me spoil your dinner, Colonel," Chase said. "I can talk and eat at the same time."

Borgnine looked at Chaffee, and O'Fallon seemed decidedly ill at ease; dining with a two-star general was not his idea of pleasant sociability.

369

"I've been reading your reports with a great deal of interest," Chase said. "As I remarked to Captain McCracken, they differ largely from the stories sent in by Mr. Dandridge."

Brubaker's eyes got round and cautious. "I hardly see how that is possible, sir. I checked the dispatches myself and they were substantially the same as . . ."

"It's no matter," Chase said. "My soup is getting cold."

"I beg the general's pardon," Brubaker said, "but it is most important to me. Surely I can't be blamed for the changes some poor editorial assistant made."

"You're not being blamed," Chase said. "But it may interest you to know that Mr. Dandridge's material came in via other means than the Fetterman telegraph."

"Really?" Brubaker had difficulty saying that. "Then unauthorized dispatches . . ."

General Chase put down his spoon.

"Colonel, I do not wish to debate the matter. I am quite familiar with the limitless excuses you seem to have at your command. If you recall I listened to them for three and a half hours once at your hearing concerning an unmentioned retreat." He sighed heavily. "However, there is a matter that I wish to discuss with you when dinner is over. Regardless of the validity of your dispatches, or Mr. Dandridge's published stories, one glaring thing remains, and I will not ignore it."

"What — what is that, sir?"

General Chase leaned forward so that he could speak softly. "Colonel, you conducted this campaign with all the instincts of a miser, sending a force this size to subdue a hostile Indian nation. You failed to give them support and you threw the bulk of the defense on an unproven weapon. In short, you jeopardized the welfare of a frontier for your own picayune reasons." His frown was like a storm ready to break. "After supper we will

371

discuss your military future, if any. Perhaps we can find a post back East somewhere where there is no action. Quartermaster duty, let's say." He held Brubaker with his glance. "You seem ill, Colonel. Perhaps you would like to be excused?"

"Yes," Brubaker said. "Yes, I would." He got up from the table and moved toward the door, but before he could touch the knob it opened and Sheila Glendennon stopped there. Her glance sought General Chase immediately.

Chase asked, "Who is this woman?"

"Lieutenant Glendennon's wife," McCracken said. "He was killed in the line of duty."

"My deepest regrets," Chase said, bowing slightly.

"I want to talk to you," Sheila said dully "You're a general and you rank a colonel, so I'll talk to you."

"Of course," Chase said gently. "What about?"

"Him," Sheila said, pointing to Truman Brubaker. "I've got a lot to say about him, General. He tried to use my husband."

"Oh?" Chase's eyebrow went up. "Perhaps in your quarters, madam. You come along too, Colonel."

Brubaker's shoulders rounded and he turned once for an instant to look at McCracken, then went out. General Lucius Chase followed him. Sheila started to close the door, then she spoke to McCracken. "This was for Harry. The only decent thing I ever did for him."

There was a profound silence in the room after the door closed. Lieutenant Finlay Chalmers broke it. "What the deuce does she mean? Is the colonel being sacked?"

Ness Barlow, who had been standing in the doorway throughout Chase's visit, hurried in with a huge tray of food. This filled the gap and Chalmer's question remained unanswered.

For an instant Ness caught McCracken's eye, then she left the room and McCracken's attention returned to the officers. He recalled his first-impression dislike of Chalmers and became determined to overcome it. Borgnine began talking about the success of artillery against a hostile force and Chalmers looked a little amused and vastly bored by it all.

"I suggest a toast," Lieutenant Chaffee said, rising. "To Captain Robert McCracken and his bride-to-be."

Everyone drank; then Lieutenant O'Fallon, who was now beginning to take the army seriously, rose. "Gentlemen, let's not forget the campaign and Captain McCracken's successful introduction of a most formidable weapon of war."

There was a murmured approval of this and the wine poured again. Each man raised his glass and toasted, all except Lieutenant Finlay Chalmers.

"Here now, Chalmers," Borgnine said. "That's hardly polite."

"I'm sorry, gentlemen. I certainly have no wish to offend Captain McCracken, nor do I wish to have my view misconstrued as something personal. But I cannot drink a toast to that, sir. Artillery, in itself, is an outdated weapon, and in a few more years it will be unheard of, except in the discussion of past campaigns."

"Well, I'll be damned," McCracken said. "Mr. Chalmers, from the first moment you set foot on this post, you've seen fit to ridicule a weapon that secured this campaign. Now I don't think it will be too much to ask if you explain your attitude."

Ness came up behind McCracken and put her hand gently on his shoulder. Lieutenant Chalmers settled back, hands lightly resting on the table. "I can understand your devotion to this arm, since you've applied so much time and energy. But I can assure you, Captain, that I am here to demonstrate a weapon that will make every other arm obsolete."

"That's nonsense," McCracken snapped. "If you think you're going to turn my post into a testing ground, you're very mistaken . . . "

"Let's see this miracle weapon," Borgnine challenged. "Please, Mr. Chalmers, purely for our enlightenment."

"Very well, then." He excused himself and went out. Talk buzzed around the table.

"What the devil is it?" McCracken asked.

Chalmers seemed to be gone an unduly long time, but it was actually only a matter of minutes. He returned with four of his men and they carried a canvas-covered affair over three feet long and equally as high.

"Just set it there," Chalmers said. Then he stood to one side and paused theatrically before withdrawing the cover. The weapon was a multi-barreled gun with a huge crank on one side, supported by a tripod that swiveled and elevated the weapon.

"This," he said, "is a Gatling machine gun. Rate of fire, over two hundred rounds of ammunition per minute. A weapon like this will enable three men to equal the fighting strength of an entire infantry company." He made a dramatic pause. "I've secured the War Department's permission to demonstrate this in the field under combat conditions."

McCracken sat like a man dumbstruck. He pointed to the gun, and said, "What kind of an idiot idea is this? Lieutenant, you can't be serious in believing that this will ever replace artillery or the rifle?"

"That is what I believe, sir. And I will prove it."

"You'll be the laughing stock of the army if you try," McCracken said. "Borgnine, you're a persuasive man; convince him."

"I couldn't interfere, sir. Department sent him here."

McCracken stared at the Gatling gun as though it were some horrible apparition. Lieutenant Chalmers said, "Captain, I realize that I'm alone in my fight but someday I'll prove that this weapon has value." He paused. "Personally, I have a great admiration for you and your views on artillery. I read your papers on the subject."

"Well, thank you," McCracken said, finding at last something to admire in this man.

"But they are antique," Chalmers added.

McCracken would have gotten to his feet if Ness had not held him back. "Mr. Chalmers, I don't think we're going to get along."

"I'm sorry to hear that. I ask only for the opportunity to test this weapon in the field."

"Oh, you shall have that," McCracken assured him.

"But will you support me?" Chalmers asked. "Captain, after the success of this campaign, you're the champion of artillery and your opinion would have great weight in Washington. If I succeed, will you place your endorsement on my report?"

McCracken stared; how familiar was

the ring of those words! He suddenly began to laugh, and the others leaned back in their chairs and roared at the paradox of it all.

Lieutenant Chalmers was positive that he had committed some unpardonable social error and stood there, embarrassed and confused. Finally McCracken controlled his laughter and wiped his eyes. He got up and offered Chalmers his hand, which was accepted a little dubiously.

"Mr. Chalmers, I'll help you prove how good this damned thing is. Sit down, man, and we'll prove it together."

Chalmers was too bewildered to speak. He gave McCracken's hand a final wring then took his place at the table.

Ness looked at McCracken, her expression puzzled. "I don't understand what was so funny, Bob."

He looked at her and smiled. "It's just the army," he said. "After you've lived with it a few years, you might think it's funny too."

"It'll be more than a few years," she said quietly.

THE END

FARGO: PANAMA GOLD
John Benteen

With foreign money behind him, Buckner was going to destroy the Panama Canal before it could be completed. Fargo's job was to stop Buckner.

FARGO: THE SHARPSHOOTERS
John Benteen

The Canfield clan, thirty strong were raising hell in Texas. Fargo was tough enough to hold his own against the whole clan.

PISTOL LAW
Paul Evan Lehman

Lance Jones came back to Mustang for just one thing — revenge! Revenge on the people who had him thrown in jail.

RIFLES ON THE RANGE
Lee Floren

Doc Mike and the farmer stood there alone between Smith and Watson. There was this moment of stillness, and then the roar would start. And somebody would die . . .

HARTIGAN
Marshall Grover

Hartigan had come to Cornerstone to die. He chose the time and the place, and Main Street became a battlefield.

SUNDANCE: OVERKILL
John Benteen

When a wealthy banker's daughter was kidnapped by the Cheyenne, he offered Sundance $10,000 to rescue the girl.

WOLF DOG RANGE
Lee Floren

Will Ardery would stop at nothing,
unless something stopped him first
— like a bullet from Pete Manly's
gun.

DEVIL'S DINERO
Marshall Grover

Plagued by remorse, a rich old
reprobate hired the Texas Troubleshooters to deliver a fortune in
greenbacks to each of his victims.

GUNS OF FURY
Ernest Haycox

Dane Starr, alias Dan Smith, wanted
to close the door on his past and
hang up his guns, but people
wouldn't let him.

GUNSLINGER'S RANGE
Jackson Cole

Three escaped convicts are out for revenge. They won't rest until they put a bullet through the head of the dirty snake who locked them behind bars.

RUSTLER'S TRAIL
Lee Floren

Jim Carlin knew he would have to stand up and fight because he had staked his claim right in the middle of Big Ike Outland's best grass.

THE TRUTH ABOUT SNAKE RIDGE
Marshall Grover

The troubleshooters came to San Cristobal to help the needy. For Larry and Stretch the turmoil began with a brawl and then an ambush.

HELL RIDERS
Steve Mensing

Wade Walker's kid brother, Duane, was locked up in the Silver City jail facing a rope at dawn. Wade was a ruthless outlaw, but he was smart, and he had vowed to have his brother out of jail before morning!

DESERT OF THE DAMNED
Nelson Nye

The law was after him for the murder of a marshal — a murder he didn't commit. Breen was after him for revenge — and Breen wouldn't stop at anything . . . blackmail, a frameup . . . or murder.

DAY OF THE COMANCHEROS
Steven C. Lawrence

Their very name struck terror into men's hearts — the Comancheros, a savage army of cutthroats who swept across Texas, leaving behind a bloodstained trail of robbery and murder.

ARIZONA DRIFTERS
W. C. Tuttle

When drifting Dutton and Lonnie Steelman decide to become partners they find that they have a common enemy in the formidable Thurston brothers.

TOMBSTONE
Matt Braun

Wells Fargo paid Luke Starbuck to outgun the silver-thieving stagecoach gang at Tombstone. Before long Luke can see the only thing bearing fruit in this eldorado will be the gallows tree.

HIGH BORDER RIDERS
Lee Floren

Buckshot McKee and Tortilla Joe cut the trail of a border tough who was running Mexican beef into Texas. They stopped the smuggler in his tracks.

FIGHTING RAMROD
Charles N. Heckelmann

Most men would have cut their losses, but Frazer counted the bullets in his guns and said he'd soak the range in blood before he'd give up another inch of what was his.

LONE GUN
Eric Allen

Smoke Blackbird had been away too long. The Lequires had seized the Blackbird farm, forcing the Indians and settlers off, and no one seemed willing to fight! He had to fight alone.

THE THIRD RIDER
Barry Cord

Mel Rawlins wasn't going to let anything stand in his way. His father was murdered, his two brothers gone. Now Mel rode for vengeance.

FARGO: MASSACRE RIVER
John Benteen

The ambushers up ahead had now blocked the road. Fargo's convoy was a jumble, a perfect target for the insurgents' weapons!

SUNDANCE: DEATH IN THE LAVA
John Benteen

The Modoc's captured the wagon train and its cargo of gold. But now the halfbreed they called Sundance was going after it . . .

HARSH RECKONING
Phil Ketchum

Five years of keeping himself alive in a brutal prison had made Brand tough and careless about who he gunned down . . .

BRETT RANDALL, GAMBLER
E. B. Mann

Larry Day had the choice of running away from the law or of assuming a dead man's place. No matter what he decided he was bound to end up dead.

THE GUNSHARP
William R. Cox

The Eggerleys weren't very smart. They trained their sights on Will Carney and Arizona's biggest blood bath began.

THE DEPUTY OF SAN RIANO
Lawrence A. Keating and
Al. P. Nelson

When a man fell dead from his horse, Ed Grant was spotted riding away from the scene. The deputy sheriff rode out after him and came up against everything from gunfire to dynamite.

SUNDANCE: SILENT ENEMY
John Benteen

A lone crazed Cheyenne was on a personal war path. They needed to pit one man against one crazed Indian. That man was Sundance.

LASSITER
Jack Slade

Lassiter wasn't the kind of man to listen to reason. Cross him once and he'll hold a grudge for years to come — if he let you live that long.

LAST STAGE TO GOMORRAH
Barry Cord

Jeff Carter, tough ex-riverboat gambler, now had himself a horse ranch that kept him free from gunfights and card games. Until Sturvesant of Wells Fargo showed up.

McALLISTER ON THE COMANCHE CROSSING
Matt Chisholm

The Comanche, McAllister owes them a life — and the trail is soaked with the blood of the men who had tried to outrun them before.

QUICK-TRIGGER COUNTRY
Clem Colt

Turkey Red hooked up with Curly Bill Graham's outlaw crew. But wholesale murder was out of Turk's line, so when range war flared he bucked the whole border gang alone . . .

CAMPAIGNING
Jim Miller

Ambushed on the Santa Fe trail, Sean Callahan is saved by two Indian strangers. But there'll be more lead and arrows flying before the band join Kit Carson against the Comanches.

DONOVAN
Elmer Kelton

Donovan was supposed to be dead. Uncle Joe Vickers had fired off both barrels of a shotgun into the vicious outlaw's face as he was escaping from jail. Now Uncle Joe had been shot — in just the same way.

CODE OF THE GUN
Gordon D. Shirreffs

MacLean came riding home, with saddle tramp written all over him, but sewn in his shirt-lining was an Arizona Ranger's star.

GAMBLER'S GUN LUCK
Brett Austen

Gamblers seldom live long. Parker was a hell of a gambler. It was his life — or his death . . .

ORPHAN'S PREFERRED
Jim Miller

Sean Callahan answers the call of the Pony Express and fights Indians and outlaws to get the mail through.

DAY OF THE BUZZARD
T. V. Olsen

All Val Penmark cared about was getting the men who killed his wife.

THE MANHUNTER
Gordon D. Shirreffs

Lee Kershaw knew that every Rurale in the territory was on the lookout for him. But the offer of $5,000 in gold to find five small pieces of leather was too good to turn down.